KILLED IN KING'S CROSS

CASSIE COBURN MYSTERY #6

SAMANTHA SILVER

BLUEBERRY BOOKS PRESS

CHAPTER 1

The knock at my door was brisk and official. It couldn't have been Violet; she never knocked. Either she texted that she was coming, or, as was more common, she simply let herself in. The fact that I kept my front door locked at all times was in no way a deterrent for her.

Getting up from my spot on the couch, where I had been casually browsing Etsy for Christmas presents on my iPad – what *do* you get a woman like Violet as a present? – my cat Biscuit meowed his disapproval as he was forced to move off my legs, where he had been comfortably snoring away.

"Sorry, buddy," I muttered as I made my way towards the front door, and shooting a look back to the couch, Biscuit had obviously decided that the warm spot I'd left was a great place to continue his nap as he had already curled himself up in it and gone back to sleep by the time I was unlocking the front door.

As soon as I opened the front door, I found myself facing an official-looking man, tall and slim, with a sour expression on his face, holding up a white card and black badge identifying him as a member of the Metropolitan Police. Behind him were two uniformed officers.

"Cassie Coburn?"

"Yes," I replied, the curiosity in my voice evident.

"Do you know the whereabouts of Violet Despuis?"

"She's not home?"

"Not at the moment."

"Then no, I don't know where she is."

"We were told you were the woman closest to her."

"Yeah, well, I'm not her mom. She's a grown woman, she can go where she wants without telling me. Frankly, I prefer it that way."

I had a feeling Violet generally got into situations that I absolutely did not want to know about.

"Are you able to get into contact with her?"

I shrugged. "I can text her."

"Well, do so."

"Why?" I asked, my eyes narrowing.

"Because a member of the Metropolitan police told you to, that's why," the man said, standing taller.

"Yeah, that's not a good enough reason," I said. "I want actual details before I'm going to bother Violet."

The man looked like he wanted to argue with me,

then eventually sighed. "There's been a murder at King's Cross, and her presence is requested to consult on the crime. Tell her DCI Kilmer requested her."

I raised my eyebrows. "At the train station?"

"Yes, at the station."

"Alright, I'll let her know," I said. "I can't guarantee she'll come."

"Good. Tell her it's urgent."

With that, the man spun on his heel and headed back towards the street, like spending an extra second with me was one more than he was willing to do.

Still, if the cops were trying this desperately to get a hold of Violet, it had to be an important murder.

I sent her a text straight away. *Murder at King's Cross Station. Police just came by asking for your help, if you can make it.*

I tossed the phone on the couch, looked over at a comfortable-looking Biscuit, who was fast asleep in my spot, sighed and leaned against the arm of the couch as I turned on the TV and switched the channel over to BBC news.

A smart-looking woman of Indian descent was reporting into the camera, the familiar scene of one of London's busiest train stations behind her one of complete chaos.

"All we've been told at the moment is that King's Cross station has been closed due to a police incident. Onlookers reported a body falling from the sky and into the main area of the station. We have no indication yet as to whether or not terrorism might be involved."

I turned off the TV and looked at Biscuit. "I figure it's probably worth going myself, don't you?"

I took the total lack of response from Biscuit to be a yes. Evidently, my presence wasn't needed here for him to have a good nap.

Grabbing a jacket – it was coming up to Christmas, after all – I made my way out of the apartment, looked up to Violet's windows, which were drawn, checked to see that she hadn't replied to my text, then ordered an Uber. Normally I would have just walked and taken the subway, but I figured if King's Cross was closed completely, then the underground was going to be complete and total chaos at best.

It turned out that traffic was just as bad; by the time the car I was in got onto Marylebone we were absolutely crawling. By the time we reached Warren Street, I gave up, thanked the driver, got out of the car and figured walking the last fifteen minutes was going to be faster than driving.

I was definitely right.

As I got closer to King's Cross station, the chaos in what was already normally a pretty chaotic place was just off the charts. News vans from dozens of stations with offices in the city were set up on the street, blocking traffic even as uniformed police officers yelled at the drivers to get out of the way. Crowds of bemused onlookers stood around, hoping for a glimmer of information or for something interesting to happen, while harried-looking men and women in suits rushed by on their phones, their plans for the day evidently disrupted by the closure of one of the biggest train stations in the world.

I wandered around the front of the station slowly, absorbing the scene all around. Yellow police tape cordoned off the entire station, with strict-looking cops stationed every few feet, making sure no daring member of the public was going to dart past to get a closer look.

"What's going on?" I asked a pleasant-looking young couple who whispered to themselves, pointing inside the station. "Any idea what's happened?"

"They've closed the whole station," the girl replied. "Never seen anything like it before."

"Apparently, someone went nuts and stabbed a bunch of people," the man replied. "That's what I've heard, anyway."

"No, dummy," the girlfriend replied with a playful nudge. "Someone killed themselves. That's what Anna texted me."

I nodded and wandered off. I really didn't know what I was doing here. After all, no one here knew me, and even if they did, there was no reason for me to be let in on the investigation. Sure, I was a little bit curious about what had happened, but that was it.

"It appears that the curiosity, it has gotten the better of you," a French accent said from behind me, and I turned and smiled at Violet. Despite the fact that it was the middle of winter and most of us looked more like the Michelin Man than normal human beings, Violet still managed to be the most elegant-looking person I'd ever met. With her long ponytail draped over one shoulder, and a long, black woolen coat covering everything except black-legginged legs and black boots, she looked like she had just walked straight out of the Paris version of this month's Vogue.

"Well, the cops seemed pretty desperate for you to come help them, so I got a bit curious," I admitted.

"Good. Then come, we will go see what this murder is all about."

I couldn't deny the fact that my heart jumped with a bit of glee at those words. For as much as I wasn't a cop, and had absolutely no detective skills whatsoever, I did enjoy joining Violet while she did her thing. It was a little bit like watching the best athlete in the field, or watching an incredible artist work: seeing Violet at a crime scene was an art in and of itself.

And, if I was completely honest, it was kind of cool getting an inside look at a scene that most people were never invited to see.

"Let's go, then," Violet said, and I scurried after her as she made her way towards the yellow cordon.

CHAPTER 2

As soon as we reached the cordon, Violet slipped under it.

"Miss Despuis," the uniformed officer told her, but then held out a hand as I went to pass. "Sorry, miss. I have strict orders to let Violet Despuis through, but no other civilians."

"Cassie's presence is invaluable to me," Violet told the man. "If you refuse to let her pass as well, I will not make myself available to assist the police. You can either let her through and tell that to your superior, or you can explain to him how you were the reason Violet Despuis did not come to help at a murder where my help is obviously badly needed."

The officer shifted from foot to foot for a minute, obviously not sure what to do, before muttering something into his radio. When, a moment later, he got an answer back, he motioned for me to follow.

Violet raised her eyebrows. "The man who cannot make a decision for himself and must rely on a superior's orders at all times is not a man who will go far in life," she told him, before striding off. I gave the guy a half-sympathetic smile – Violet could be very cutting when she wanted to be – and continued on after her.

Before we even reached the front door, the same tall man who had been at my apartment came over towards her. Without even acknowledging my presence, he began to tell Violet about the case.

"The first calls to 999 came in at two minutes to two this afternoon. CCTV footage shows the man falling one minute before that. Victim is a thirty-year old male, local."

"And why am I here?"

"The sheer magnitude of this thing. It's going to be all over the news, around the world. We might be dealing with a serial killer, here."

"So you do not want my help so much as you are ensuring that should anyone question your investigation you can tell them that you have hired me to help with the case."

"Well, um, your help is considered valuable," the man muttered, and I hid a smile. It was obvious Violet had just hit the nail on the head.

"No matter. You will not have to face difficult questions if you allow me to help, as I will find your killer. Now, take me to the body."

The man dutifully led us along Pancras Road,

through the entrance, and into a half-moon-shaped area lined with shops. I'd had an absolutely God-awful spelt and quinoa scone at one of the shops here after Violet had dissuaded me away from the much more appetizing chocolate croissants. I didn't know King's Cross *super* well, but I had been here a few times. Obviously, I had to take a selfie at the platform 9 3/4 , and I may have spent a little bit of cash at the souvenir shop down the hall as well.

But now, I was here for an entirely different reason. This entrance was rather ornate: directly in front of us was the brick façade of the old train station, with a modern, white diamond-patterned funnel leading the eye. In the center of that funnel was a body surrounded by broken glass. The man was dressed well, in slacks and a fancy jacket, with a scarf spread around him. There was only a little bit of blood near the body.

My focus wasn't immediately on the body, though. Instead, my focus turned to a smartly-dressed man hunched over the body, his face focused and full of concentration as he inspected it.

"Jake!" I said, and the man looked up, his features breaking into a grin.

"Cassie. Fancy seeing you here."

I made my way over to my boyfriend, one of the pathologists for the city. Jake Edmunds looked more like he belonged on a beach in Australia than the middle of a murder investigation in London, with his sandy blond hair and muscular build.

"What's happened here?"

"He fell through the roof," Jake deadpanned, motioning to the glass around us. I looked up to the ceiling. Sure enough, one of the large, rectangular glass panels above was missing its pane. Looking closely at the man, his face was covered in cuts from where he had gone through the glass.

I frowned. That wasn't right; someone who had jumped through a pane of glass should have gone feet first. Or, at the very least, he would have instinctively protected his face. And yet, his arms seemed to be relatively cut-free, at least compared to his face.

"He was killed before he jumped," I said to Jake, who nodded.

"Yeah. His face wouldn't be that cut up if he'd been alive. Besides, who kills themselves by going headfirst through a pane of glass?"

"Someone who wants to be really sure it worked?" I offered, and Jake gave me a grim smile.

"Well, whoever did this definitely made sure it worked," he replied. "Because this guy was killed before he hit the ground, one hundred percent."

"Do you know what the cause of death is, yet?" I glanced around the body; there were no obvious marks that might indicate the cause of death, like a gunshot wound, or having his head bashed in.

"Strangulation," Jake replied with a nod. I took a pair of latex gloves Jake handed me wordlessly, slipped them on, then moved the collar of the man's jacket carefully. Sure enough, a belt-shaped purple bruise around his neck was a pretty good indicator of the cause of death.

"Petechial hemorrhaging confirms it," Jake said as my eyes widened slightly at the sight of the bruise.

"Yup, that'll do it. Sending him through the glass was definitely overkill."

"Or it was done on purpose, as a display," Violet said from behind us.

"Someone showing off?" I asked, and she nodded.

"Yes. In fact, I think it incredibly likely."

"How do you know?" I asked, looking over the man once more. After all, I knew about the medicine – though it wasn't too difficult to figure out that a guy with a giant bruise on his neck had been strangled – but how on earth Violet knew more than that was beyond me.

"Well, to begin, look at where the body has been dumped. This man was not dropped in a back alley behind a non-descript building. He was not dumped in the Thames with the hopes that his body would be washed to sea before being discovered. No, he was dropped headlong into the center of London, in what is arguably the busiest part of the city at any given moment. And on top of that, look at the man's shoes."

I looked down towards the feet, and my eyes widened. "They're too big for him!"

"And not simply by one half a size, or something similar. Those shoes are at least two sizes too large. His jacket as well, it does not fit him, despite being of good quality. It is much too loose in the shoulders."

I looked over the man more carefully; I wanted to see if I could spot anything myself. "His hands... his fingers, they're quite dirty," I said, and Violet nodded.

"Yes, it has been quite some time since this man has last bathed. I presume that he is, in fact, homeless. The nice clothes, the location chosen, it has all been to create a certain spectacle."

As I looked closer at the man, I could see Violet was definitely right. Not only were his fingers dirty, but a few of the cuts on his face were too straight, like they were shaving nicks. Someone giving this man a bad shave would have definitely done it. His hair was quite greasy, as well, despite the decent-looking haircut.

"Do you think it might be terrorism?" I asked, my mind turning back to the words of the BBC reporter, but Violet shook her head.

"No, I do not think that. For a terrorist, it would not matter what the person looked like. The only thing that would be important would be that people be scared that it could happen to them as well. A man who was able to get a body to the roof of this building without anyone noticing, and was able to get away after dropping the body to the ground, is a man who could have easily dropped a bomb, which would have caused far more chaos and terror. No, I do not believe this was terrorism."

"We don't believe it either," DCI Kilmer said,

making his way towards us. In his hand was a sealed plastic envelope, the type the police used to preserve evidence. "This was found on the body."

Violet looked at the note, then handed it over to me.

Hickory dickory dock.

The note was printed on regular paper, as far as I could tell, in Times New Roman font. It couldn't have looked more generic if it tried. I passed the note over to Jake, whose eyebrows rose when he read it, then he passed it back on to Violet.

"We don't know what this means just yet," DCI Kilmer said.

"Have you identified the man?" Violet asked.

"Not as of yet. We're running the man's fingerprints through the system now in the hopes of getting a match, but a well-dressed man like this? I doubt he's ever been arrested."

A hint of a smile flittered on Violet's lips. "I believe you will find this gentleman was homeless, DCI."

"Homeless? A man dressed in shoes that cost two hundred pounds, at least?"

"A man dressed in two hundred pound shoes that are two sizes too big for him, yes," Violet replied. "I cannot say whether or not this man has been arrested before, but he is not an ordinary rich citizen of this great city."

DCI Kilmer puzzled over the body for a while as Violet moved from the corpse lying in front of us and began looking around, and then up.

"How did the killer manage to get around the security here?" Violet asked, and DCI Kilmer glowered.

"Believe me, I've asked the same question of the head of security."

"I would like to speak with him myself," Violet said, and DCI Kilmer nodded before speaking quickly into his radio.

"He'll be here in a moment."

Violet was definitely getting the VIP treatment here today; the police must have wanted this case solved fast. Usually, whenever members of the Metropolitan Police had to interact with Violet – and I say 'had' because only DCI Williams ever seemed to do it willingly – they were indifferent at best, insulting at worst. The vast, vast majority of the members of the force were not appreciative of Violet, and to be totally honest, I could see why. She didn't exactly hide her feelings when it came to cops: namely, that most of them were completely incompetent and that they managed to solve any crimes at all was more a matter of luck than good detective work.

So the fact that DCI Kilmer was being so gracious to Violet told me one thing: they definitely wanted this case solved, and fast.

I couldn't blame them. This was already a media gong show.

CHAPTER 3

The head of security at King's Cross station was brought over a few moments later. He was tall, burly, with a smattering of red hair on top of his equally red face.

"You are the head of security?" Violet asked him, and he nodded a little bit *too* enthusiastically. I had a sneaking suspicion he had a feeling it was one of the last times he was going to be able to give that as his job title.

"Yes, that's me. John Montgomery's my name. I know, we've made a mess of things."

"Tell me, how was a mess made? Was there security footage on the roof of the station?"

The man shook his head. "We never thought we'd need it there, to be quite honest. A bit of a stuff up, in retrospect."

"Yes, I would agree," Violet muttered. "Do you know

how the man was able to gain access to the roof without any witnesses? It would not have been simple, dragging a dead body up there."

"I'm going to be honest with you, we haven't the slightest."

Violet raised her eyebrows. "Really? You do not have any idea how the man could have got up onto the roof?"

Montgomery shrugged his shoulders. "I don't know what to tell you. We've never had any sort of incident like this before. Look, I can take you to our control station, where you can see all of the CCTV footage we've got, but that's all I can offer you I'm afraid. There's no footage on the roofs at all."

Violet nodded. "I would like to see that, please."

I waved a goodbye to Jake, who grinned at me in return as Violet and I made our way to the main security office, followed closely by DCI Kilmer, who obviously wanted to glean any bits of insight Violet might have to offer.

I had to admit, as soon as we entered the clinical-looking room, I was fairly surprised by the sheer volume of cameras. I didn't know why; I knew King's Cross, being such a hotbed of people in a city famed for the spying it does on its citizens, would be filled with security cameras. Sure enough, dozens of monitors lined the far wall, showing every single inch of every single tunnel and platform inside this extensive network of rail lines.

I spotted three monitors showing the spot where Jake was still busily looking over the body, though he was only in the center frame of one of them. In front of the monitors were three rows of desks, each of which were manned by at least four people, all of them wearing headsets into which they mumbled every so often.

No one even looked up when the four of us entered. Montgomery led us to an empty desk at the far end of the room, where he turned on the black monitor.

"This will give you access to all of the videos from the past thirty days, which we keep on the servers. Anything from earlier than that is accessible, but is in cold storage and would require twenty-four hours' notice to bring online."

"This should be fine, thank you," Violet replied with a curt nod as she seated herself down in the chair in front of the monitor.

"I can show you how it wor-" Montgomery started, then stopped as Violet had already begun tapping away at the keys and bringing up various views. "Never mind, you seem to have the hang of it."

"I have done this before here, once or twice, but not for quite a few years," Violet explained without looking up from the screen. I watched as she brought up a number of different views of the station earlier that day. I didn't know if Violet could see anything I didn't – she almost always did, after all – but as far as I could tell, nothing suspicious was happening on any of the screens. No one looked like they were dragging a body through the halls or anything like that.

In fact, up until the moment when the body came plunging through the ceiling and everyone scrambled to get away, there was absolutely no indication as far as I could tell that anything was wrong.

"Do you see anything?" I asked Violet, and she shook her head.

"No. I do not, as of yet. However, I would like to have the previous seven days' worth of video from all cameras downloaded onto a hard drive for me to look at from home later."

"Consider it done," Montgomery replied, striding over to one of the security personnel and whispering into their ear.

Violet leaned back in her chair.

"It really would interest me to know how the man got onto the roof."

"Why?" DCI Kilmer replied. "We've got teams up there now, checking for fingerprints. What does it matter how he got up there? All we need to know is that he did."

If Violet had planned on hiding her contempt, she failed completely. "It is important because it is crucial to the case. Someone who manages to get a human body on the roof of King's Cross Station without being caught on CCTV footage is not an amateur. Also, I would like copies of the footage from all CCTV cameras in a one hundred meter radius from this station for the previous week sent to me as well."

"Right, I'll have an officer bring it by to you later."

"Good," Violet nodded, getting up from her chair. "Well, thank you gentlemen, that will be all for today."

I followed after Violet and we made our way out of the station.

"So you really didn't see anything on that camera?"

"No," Violet said. "Although, to be honest, I did not expect to. Someone who managed to commit this crime without getting caught is someone who knew what they were doing. As much as the television and popular culture enjoys the portrayal of the accidental perfect crime, in reality, it does not happen. I would be surprised if it was the first crime this person had committed."

"I'm guessing you're thinking the cops aren't going to find any fingerprints on the roof, then," I offered, and Violet shook her head.

"No, they will not. However, I do want to know how the man got onto the roof."

The two of us made our way out, and I looked around. "There?" I suggested, pointing to a white-and-brown brick building next to the station. The sign above it read 'Great Northern Hotel'. The windows on the eastern side of the building led directly onto the roof of the train station.

"Perfect," Violet said quietly with a nod, and the two of us made our way towards the entrance. "Very good deduction," she added as we passed back under the police line and out of the restricted area. A small blush crept up my face; I was definitely not a detective, but it was nice when I noticed things and Violet recognized them.

The two of us made our way towards the ledge, and looked up.

"I mean, it wouldn't have been super discreet," I said, suddenly thinking my idea might not have been the best. While a handful of windows seemed to look directly over the roof, they were also in plain view of anyone walking or driving past.

"That is true," Violet said slowly. "Can you text Jake and ask him if he has a time of death, yet?"

"Sure," I said, pulling out my phone and typing a text as we made our way to the hotel's front door. By the time we reached the entrance, I had gotten a reply.

"He says either late last night or early this morning, but he won't have a more precise time of death until he gets back to the lab."

"Good," Violet nodded, and we made our way through the hotel's front doors.

The lobby was small, with a narrow hallway leading to the main reception desk, but tastefully decorated. I imagined the rooms were tiny, but in a location like this, I imagined it was still at least hundreds of pounds a night to stay here.

A friendly-looking woman with her hair tied smartly back smiled at us as we reached reception.

"Good morning, how can I help you?"

"Hello, I am wondering if I could have access to a list of your guests who have occupied the suites that overlook the roof of the train station for the previous week," Violet asked.

The friendly-but-indifferent smile on the woman's face turned into a falsely sympathetic smile.

"I'm sorry, but that goes against our hotel policy."

"Have you seen all of the police officers outside? They are currently attempting to solve a murder, one which may have taken place in this very hotel."

The woman's face paled slightly, but she wasn't moved. "I'm afraid without a warrant from the police, I cannot give you that information."

"Fine," Violet said, pulling out her phone. "I will call and have a warrant issued. However, I am certain that in press releases the police would much prefer talking about the co-operative Great Northern Hotel rather than bemoaning the lack of co-operation received during one of the most high-profile murders England has ever seen."

At this, the woman paused. "Hold on. Let me get my manager."

She darted out from behind the desk and made her way into a back office. Violet smiled at me.

"Judging by that look, I'm guessing that there's not nearly enough proof to actually get a warrant for that information?"

"You are really starting to get to know me well,"

Violet replied. "The fact that there is a possibility that the killer got onto the roof via the hotel is absolutely not enough for a warrant. And to be completely honest, it absolutely should not be."

"That's probably true," I laughed, just as the woman came back with another woman, this time older, short and slim.

"Are you ladies with the police?" the woman asked, looking us up and down.

"I am working with the police on this case," Violet replied.

"You are Violet Despuis." The woman said it as much more statement than question.

"I am, yes."

"Right. Well, while it is highly unusual to hand over such information without a warrant, I think in this case we can make an exception, especially for someone of your reputation. I know there are data protection laws, but protection of the public I think is more important."

"Thank you," Violet replied.

"Cara, please get these ladies the information they're after," the woman said, before turning and making her way back into her office. It turned out the name Violet Despuis still opened doors.

Or, in this case, records.

"Just one second, and let me get the information you requested," Cara said to us as she strode back over to her computer and typed away efficiently. "You don't really think the person was killed in this hotel, were they?"

"At this point, I do not know for certain, but it cannot be ruled out. I believe it likely that if nothing else, the body has passed through these doors."

Cara shook her head while making a bit of a tusk-tusk noise. I wasn't sure if she thought it was a shame for the victim, or for the hotel.

"Do you have cameras in the hotel as well?" Violet asked, looking around.

"Of course."

"Would I be able to get a copy of the previous week's cameras from this lobby?"

"I can do that," Cara said. "We have one angle here that covers the entire hallway. Anyone entering or leaving the hotel will be caught by that camera, except for those leaving through the service entrance."

"That would be excellent, thank you," Violet said.

"Here is the list of names you wanted," Cara said, grabbing a piece of paper from the printer and handing it over to Violet. "If the two of you want to wait around here, either in the lobby or in the bar, I'll have security make you a copy of the tapes and bring it over to you."

"Thank you, you have been very helpful," Violet said. "I will make sure your co-operation will be duly noted."

CHAPTER 4

The two of us made our way towards a couple of white leather chairs in front of a small table. Violet moved her chair to be next to mine, and put the sheet on the table so we could look over it.

The leftmost column had a list of dates, sorted from oldest to newest, and so my eyes immediately scanned down to the bottom of the page.

There were four names on the list that had stayed in the rooms overlooking the roofs last night: Mr. Walter Knight, Dr. Johann Persson, Mrs. Eloise McMillan, and Mr. Kristoffer Lanucci. There were addresses listed for each of them, as well as phone numbers.

"Well, it probably would have been easier if one of them had checked in as Lee Harvey Oswald or something," I joked. "None of these names scream 'murderer' to me."

"I did not realize you wanted the murderer handed

to you on a platter," Violet said, raising her eyebrows slightly. "Unfortunately for you, that is rarely how the world works. Come. Let us go and see if any of these four people are currently in their rooms."

The first door we knocked on, that belonging to Mr. Kristoffer Lanucci, led to no response. Violet shrugged, and we went to the next door over. Mrs. Eloise McMillan was a heavyset woman in her fifties, with a jolly face, the type that I half-expected to invite us in for cookies and a cup of tea as soon as she saw us.

"Why, hello there," she said to us when she answered the door. "What can I do for you?"

"Hello, Mrs. McMillan. I am Violet Despuis, and this is my co-worker, Cassie Coburn. We are assisting the police with their investigation of the murder at the train station, and we were wondering if we could ask you a few questions?"

Eloise McMillan's face fell as soon as Violet said the word 'murder'.

"A murder? Here? You're joking!"

"Unfortunately, I am not."

"Well, I know your face from the telly, Violet. If you're on the case, then obviously the police are going to find out who did it. Please, come in, both of you. I'll help in any way I can."

She led us into the small suite and motioned for Violet and I to take the two chairs next to a small desk while she sat on the bed. Half the bed was now covered with bags bearing the Harrods of London logo on them. "Sorry, I haven't even got a cup of tea, or biscuits to offer you."

"That is alright, Mrs. McMillan," Violet said, while I hid a small smile.

"Please, call me Eloise. Now, what's this about a murder?"

"A man has been killed, and his body dropped into the main part of King's Cross station."

"Oh my goodness, that's just awful," Eloise said, a hand rising to her mouth. "Who would do such a thing?"

"That is what we are trying to figure out. Now, I would like to start by asking you why it is you are staying here, at this hotel in particular?"

"Well, it's just such a good location, isn't it? I'm visiting from Birmingham, as I found I don't get to London as much as I'd like to. So, I thought with it being December and all, I'd take the opportunity to get some Christmas shopping done, and King's Cross on the tube gets you anywhere you want to go in town, so it's quite convenient."

Violet nodded. "Yes, that it is. Have you left your room at all today?"

"Of course, yes. I went out just this morning and spent most of the day in Harrods. I found the loveliest Christmas ornaments, and some things for my youngest, who just bought a home with her husband."

"And when did you get back?" Violet asked.

"Oh, around an hour and a half ago, I'd say. Something like that."

Looking at my watch, I did some mental math. Ninety minutes ago would have been around fifteen minutes before the body had been found. That certainly was cutting it close.

"Did you hear or see anyone on this floor when you came back to your room?" Violet asked. Eloise thought for a moment, then shook her head.

"No, I can't say I did."

"What about last night? Were there any sounds, or anything that struck you as being out of the ordinary?"

Eloise laughed. "My dear, I come from a small suburb outside of Birmingham. To me, every sound in London is out of the ordinary. I've heard sirens outside for the last hour, and I thought for sure they were just from normal day-to-day life here, I'd no idea someone had been murdered right outside my window."

"Alright, thank you, Eloise," Violet said, and the two of us got up. Just as we made our way back into the hallway, however, Eloise stopped us.

"One moment," she said. "It may be nothing, but in the middle of the night last night I heard a thud that I thought woke me up. Or at least, I thought I had. I may have simply dreamt it, or something like that."

"At what time was that?" Violet asked, her eyes gleaming with excitement.

"It was just after two. I remember checking the clock to see the time."

"I suppose you do not know where the thud came from?"

"Sorry, no. As I said, I was half asleep, and I can't even be certain that's what I heard. Sorry I can't be more help."

"That's fine, you have been very helpful," Violet said, and as soon as Eloise shut the door behind us, Violet turned to me, a smile on her face.

"I believe we are in the right area," Violet said. "The body must have been taken through the hotel and dropped through the window onto the roof of the train station in the middle of the night."

"And it was just sitting there until two this afternoon?" I asked.

"Yes. What reason would someone have to go onto the roof of King's Cross station? Leaving a body there for twelve hours carries small risk of it being discovered, especially if it was put in a rather discreet location until the killer decided to drop it through the roof. If the body was put up there in the middle of the night, the odds of being seen are lower, and simply covering it with a tarp or something similar would have prevented any calls to 9-9-9 from people in nearby buildings who might spot it."

I nodded slowly. "That's actually rather ingenious."

"It is also why I believe we are not dealing with a killer for whom this is his or her first victim," Violet said. "Everything about this is too organized. It is too perfect."

"Serial killer?"

"I believe so."

"But why do something so obvious, then?" I asked. "I mean, if they've been killing before, presumably they haven't been caught, or they'd be in jail. So why not keep going like they're going?"

"A lot of serial killers crave attention," Violet replied. "My suspicion is that this man – or woman, though statistically it is far less likely – is attempting to goad the police, to show them how much better he is than them."

"Like the Zodiac killer."

"Exactly like that."

I nodded. That made sense. "Alright. So if TV and my basic psych courses have taught me anything, it's that one thing is certain: if this is a serial killer, he's going to strike again."

"Yes," Violet replied. "We are absolutely working against a clock right now."

On that note, we knocked on the door next to Eloise's, where Doctor Johann Persson had been staying. Again, no response. We moved to the last door, where Mr. Walter Knight was the registered guest, and found that once more, there was no answer.

"We will have to return when it is more likely that the room's occupants are here," Violet said. "Come, let us go back to the lobby and get the copy of the security footage, and we can go back to my house and look it over."

As the doors to the elevator opened, a tall, thin man with red hair who looked to be in his forties stepped out, giving Violet and I a small smile as he passed. The two of us stepped into the elevator, but just as the doors were about to close completely, Violet stuck her arm into the middle of them, opening them once more.

"What's going on?" I asked, and she pointed.

"Look into which room the man is going."

Sure enough, the man was entering the room of Doctor Johann Persson, one of the guests on our list. We stepped out of the elevator as Violet called out. "Excuse me?"

The man stopped, the door to his room half-open. "Yes?" he asked, a slight lilt to his accent. Going by the name, I figured he must have been Swedish.

"Are you Doctor Persson?"

"That is me, yes."

"I am working with the police, with regards to the murder at King's Cross station, and I am wondering if my friend and I could ask you a few questions."

"Of course. If you would like, I could meet you at the hotel restaurant in a few minutes. It has been a long few days, and I really could use a drink."

"Yes, not a problem," Violet replied, and the two of us made our way back down to ground level and into the GNH bar, where we sat at a wooden table while waiting for Doctor Persson to arrive. I looked at the menu longingly, especially when I saw how good the food looked, but realized that this was probably not going to be a long conversation, and that Violet probably wouldn't be super impressed if I took some time off from our hunt for a probable serial killer to eat some food.

About five minutes later, the doctor made his way down, ordered from the bar, and then brought a beer over as he sat down across from us.

"My apologies. It has been a long trip."

"Where are you visiting from?" Violet asked.

"Stockholm," Doctor Perrson replied. "I am here for a medical conference. As I returned from the conference I was attending, I saw what was happening outside. I assume that is the murder you are investigating?"

"That is correct," Violet replied. "Which conference are you attending?"

"It is one for oncologists, which is my specialty," the doctor replied. "In fact, the last events of the conference took place this afternoon. That is why I am enjoying this beer, then tomorrow I will spend the day sightseeing before returning to Sweden."

"Did you spend last night in your hotel room?" Violet asked.

"Well, of course, but I didn't get in until late," Doctor Persson replied. "A number of colleagues and I had a late dinner followed by drinks that went well into the night. After getting my wallet stolen during the first day of the conference, I was ready to let loose a little bit, and I didn't get in until four this morning."

"And today? You only just got back now?"

"That's right. The final presentations ended at three this afternoon. Luckily, they didn't start until noon, or I'm not sure I would have gotten out of bed in time," he added with a self-deprecating smile. Doctor Persson was definitely charming.

"When you say you had your wallet stolen," Violet continued. "Was your hotel room key in it?"

"Of course," Doctor Persson nodded. "But it's not as though the person could have used it. The cards are blank, and there was nothing in my wallet saying where I was staying. It could have been a card for any of thousands of hotel rooms in the city."

Violet nodded slowly, as Doctor Persson continued. "Besides, nothing was taken from my room. Why are you asking, anyway?"

"Oh, it is probably nothing," Violet replied with a wave of her hand, but I could see from the concentrated look in her eyes that it was most definitely not 'nothing'.

Violet had an idea. I could see it in her eyes. "Alright, thank you, *docteur*," Violet said, getting up and shaking the man's hand. "I wish you safe travels back to Sweden."

"And I wish you luck in finding your murderer," Doctor Persson replied. "I only wish that I could have been more helpful."

"You have been very helpful, thank you," Violet said, and the two of us made our way back to the front desk, where Cara had a USB drive filled with security footage ready for us.

"Here's the footage you asked for," she said, handing it over to Violet. "I do hope this murder has nothing to do with this hotel."

"Do not worry," Violet said. "If it has, I do not think there is anything anyone here could have done to prevent it."

I smiled at a noticeably relieved Cara as the two of us left the hotel, with Violet hailing a cab to take us back to Eunston Road.

"Do you want to come in and join me as we look at the tapes of the hotel?" Violet asked.

"Sure, why not?" I replied. After all, it wasn't like I had much else to do at home. I had to make a decision about whether or not I was going to go back to medical school this week, and that was a decision I was happily going to be a child about and keep putting off.

Violet gave me a look, like she knew exactly why I was coming with her, but she didn't say anything. Knowing her, she had almost certainly figured it out.

But hey, it was my decision to procrastinate about.

CHAPTER 5

"If I'm going to sit here and keep watching hours of video where literally nothing happens, then I'm ordering Chinese food," I declared three hours later. My original suggestion of doing the same had been shot down on the basis that Chinese food was "unhealthy" and "artery-clogging".

Ok, so that was totally correct. But at this point, my mind was starting to swim and I couldn't bring myself to care about anything except that sweet, sweet MSG flowing through my veins.

Violet rolled her eyes. "How on earth did you manage to complete a full education when you obviously have the attention span of a goldfish?"

"It's not that *my* attention span is bad, it's that you're a freak of nature," I replied as I pulled out my phone and opened up my favorite food delivery app.

"Anyway, I'm getting Kung Pao chicken, do you want anything?"

"Digestion interrupts the activity of the brain," Violet replied. "I will have a light meal, most likely a smoothie, to keep my body powered but prevent the post-heavy-meal sleepiness."

"You mean a food coma," I replied.

"Of course there would be a name for that," Violet sighed. "So to answer you, no, I do not want anything, thank you."

"Don't worry, I already placed the order," I grinned. "I haven't seen anything that sticks out to me in the videos, how about you?"

"No," Violet admitted with a sigh. "I, unfortunately, have not." We had started by looking at the videos from right before 2pm. The focus had been on the angle at the front of the building, where we could see anyone going in and out. We watched the video in reverse, and I had to admit, after two hours, my eyes were sore and I was starting to feel like we weren't getting anywhere.

"Can't we just play 'spot the hooker' instead?" I yawned at one point, and Violet scoffed.

"That is easy. Her, her, and also her," she said in the course of about a minute. Great.

"Now if only we could spot the murderer that easily."

Twenty minutes later, the ring of the doorbell downstairs told me my food was ready. I made my way down and grabbed the bag, basically sticking my face in the brown paper as I headed back into the study, but quickly found myself distracted. Violet had noticed something. She was now sitting on the edge of her chair, her fingers moving the video back to a certain point.

"Him," she said triumphantly, and I looked over at who she meant.

"The man with the suitcase?"

"Yes, exactly. He is the one," Violet said.

"But how do you know?" I asked, squinting at the screen. To be honest, the video quality wasn't great to begin with, and the man's face was covered with a baseball cap. I could tell he was a man, he had short hair, and he probably cheered for Manchester United. That was about it.

"Look at the suitcase."

"Ok, so he's carrying a suitcase. It's big, and it's black, and it looks like every single other suitcase out there."

"Two things: one, he is not *carrying* the suitcase, he is *rolling* the suitcase. There is a significant difference. Even when he goes to the elevator, he rolls the suitcase directly inside of it. He does not lift it for a single second. Secondly, while it looks like every other suitcase out there, it does not look like every other suitcase of the clientele of this hotel. The key selling point to a hotel in a location such as this one is its prominence to the train station, and as such, it finds its main clientele to be business travelers – the sorts of people who do not carry more than a small bag with them at one time."

"So you think there's a body in that suitcase," I said, my eyes widening slightly.

"I do," Violet nodded. "I believe that is how the man got the body upstairs."

"And you think he had Doctor Persson's room key?"

"Yes," Violet nodded. "The fact that he had his wallet stolen I do not think is a coincidence. I think the killer targeted him, took his wallet, and when he knew the *docteur* would be at the conference, he brought the body into the room, moved it onto the roof of the train station, and came back today to finish his performance."

"That's insane," I said, shaking my head. "And so incredibly risky."

"It is another reason why I do not believe this was this man's first murder. An amateur would have made mistakes. This man knew perfectly what to do. He knew where the cameras were, he knew how to shield his identity, and he has made it as difficult as possible for us to track him."

"So what's next? We have to figure out the man's identity?"

"That is correct," Violet replied. "I think that if the police had his fingerprints on file, they would have got a match already. That means we should assume that he has never been arrested, and therefore that they do not know who he is any more than we do. Grab your jacket, Cassie. We are going to pay a visit to your boyfriend. He may be able to help us identify our victim."

CHAPTER 6

*E*ven though it was now almost nine at night, Jake was still at the morgue, working away. I wasn't surprised; whenever there were major murders in London – and this definitely qualified – everyone involved in law enforcement seemed to put in the extra hours to catch the killer as soon as was humanly possible. In a case like this, which was already plastered all over the news, the police not only wanted to be able to catch the killer as quickly as they could, but they also wanted to prevent as much criticism of their management of the case as possible.

No one wanted to be the one to answer questions about why an autopsy wasn't done immediately because the pathologist wanted to go get a pint at five o'clock on the dot.

That was why, when Violet and I made our way

down into the morgue just before nine, Jake simply smiled at us as we came in.

"Come for another look?" he asked. "I've just finished the autopsy, but my preliminary report won't be ready for another twenty-four hours. But then, you've never waited for the reports."

"That is correct," Violet said. "I need to know the time of death, and I need to see the body as well. I assume there were no personal effects that belonged to the man himself?"

Jake shrugged. "No idea. That's your department, not mine. I can tell you he died between seven and nine o'clock last night, give or take half an hour. And I can tell you that his personal effects are in the cardboard box over there, but as to whether or not they actually belong to him? No idea."

Violet made her way over to the box while I headed towards Jake, while he finished sewing up the Y-incision he had made in the victim's chest.

"Long day, I guess?" I said, and Jake laughed.

"No kidding. I'm pretty sure my boss had an aneurism from the stress earlier today. How did you get involved in this, anyway?"

"The cops came to my door when they were looking for Violet in a desperate attempt to get her to help them."

Jake raised his eyebrows. "Well, that shows just how important a case this must be."

"That's what I thought," I laughed. "And since I'm

procrastinating when it comes to deciding what I'm going to do about finishing medical school, I figured I would tag along and see what happens. So far, we've figured out how he got the body onto the roof, and that we're probably looking at a serial killer."

"How *did* the body get onto the roof?" Jake asked. "I was wondering that myself. Surely, someone would have seen it. And don't think I've just skipped by the part where you're procrastinating about your medical school decision. If you need to talk about it, I'm here. It doesn't matter how busy I am with work, I will always make time to talk to you."

"Thanks," I replied gratefully. A part of me was pretty sure I was going to take Jake up on that offer. I obviously was getting absolutely nowhere making this decision on my own, and a decision did need to be made. But, that was a problem for future Cassie to deal with. For now, I was helping Violet find a serial killer. "It looks like the killer stole the wallet of a person staying at the hotel that overlooks the roof of King's cross station. Last night he took the body up to the suitcase, waited until two in the morning, then moved the body onto the roof and, we assume, hid it until he dropped it through the glass ceiling."

Jake let out a low whistle. "Wow, that's quite something."

"Serial killers often are," Violet said. "That is one of the reasons why we need to figure out the man's identity. The video from the hotel does not help us in the least; the man has hidden himself too well from the camera. He knows how to blend into a crowd, and he knows how to avoid being seen."

"Have you found anything?" I asked, but Violet shook her head.

"No, I do not believe that any of the items of clothing the man was wearing were his. As they are all quite expensive, and all are far better quality than a homeless man in this city could possibly afford."

"I thought that was strange when I got him onto the table and undressed him," Jake replied. "I'm no fashion expert or anything like that, but it was pretty obvious to me as well that this was a well-dressed man."

Violet made her way towards the body and began inspecting it.

"There has to be a hint as to who this man is here," Violet said. "Otherwise, I am afraid that I will be completely at a loss for clues, and will have no choice but to wait for this man's next victim, and hope that that time the killer will have made more mistakes."

To be completely honest, I could barely fathom a world in which Violet was unable to determine anything about a person. She was so incredibly obser-vant that sometimes a part of me wondered if she didn't have secret magical powers. Okay, that was ridiculous, but her powers of observation were really second to none.

I watched as Violet looked over every inch of the man's body.

"Did you wash anything off of him?" she asked Jake, and he nodded.

"Sure. There was definitely a layer of dust and dirt on him. It had been quite a while since this man had seen a shower, obviously."

Violet frowned. "This is going to be more difficult than I thought."

My heart dropped. "There's really nothing that can give you any hint as to his identity?"

"I did not say that," Violet said to me, shooting me a look that said I should have known better. "I simply expected it to be easier to discover this man's origin."

"What have you found?" I asked.

"There is a tattoo on his shoulder," Violet said, and I made my way over to where she pointed. Sure enough, on the back of the shoulder blade, a small tattoo of a heart made of rope, with the center of the rope turning into a noose. While it was small, the tattoo was obviously of good quality. "I recognize the work of the artist who drew this," she continued, taking out her phone and snapping a quick picture of the tattoo. "We can go and pay her a visit now; her shop will have opened for the night not long ago."

I raised my eyebrows slightly. I never felt so old as when I wondered what kind of person decided to open their business late at night. Ten o'clock was for sleeping, not for starting off the day. Yep, I was definitely an old grandmother at heart.

"I'll call you tomorrow if I can," Jake said to me as

we got ready to leave. "No guarantees, though. I'm pretty sure the boss is going to want me to have the full report on this done as fast as possible."

"No problem," I said, giving Jake a quick kiss before heading back towards the elevators.

"Don't think I haven't forgotten about your medical school applications," he added, wagging a finger at me. "You don't necessarily need to do it, but you do need to make a decision."

"I know," I said, my heart dropping slightly in my chest. I knew that I was going to have to make a decision. The problem was, I was petrified that I was going to make the wrong one.

~

About twenty minutes later, Violet and I were standing in front of the trendy little shop in the West End that took up a tiny shop space at the corner intersection between two streets. The blue brick exterior didn't look like much, but directly across the street from the spot was a gorgeous graffiti mural of an ancient Greek or Roman statue, showing signs of the neighborhood's newfound trendiness. Even though it was now almost eleven o'clock, crowds of young partygoers and clubbers roamed the streets, getting ready for a night of excitement and drinking.

The sign above the entrance to the tattoo parlor read 'Tyger Tattoos', and the windows had been tinted so that no one looking could see what was going on. It wasn't exactly the most inviting place in the world, but then again, I thought that about most tattoo parlors.

It wasn't that I had anything against tattoos; I had actually considered getting one at one point, but simply never got around to it. Plus, while I wasn't afraid of needles, I wasn't a huge fan of pain and after my accident had experienced enough of it for a lifetime. I wasn't sure I wanted to go through a lot of pain willingly just to decorate my body.

"Come," Violet said, dragging me out of my reverie, and the two of us made for the entrance.

I wasn't sure exactly what to expect when I entered, that this space looked absolutely incredible. Clean and modern, the walls were painted an extremely bright turquoise, and covered with black-framed pictures of available art. Against a far wall was a hanging rack that displayed dozens of other potential designs. The doors and trim were all painted black as well, which was striking against the bold walls.

In the middle of the room was a black table surrounded by black benches, with a few scattered sheets of paper set atop it. Against the far wall was a huge leather couch, on which lounged a woman who looked almost exactly like Kat Von D. Her arms were covered in ink, her dyed black hair was stylized to make it look huge, and her lips were a ruby red that belonged on a magazine cover. As soon as we walked in, she looked up, and those fiery red lips broke into a huge smile.

"Violet," she exclaimed in a California accent, which seemed a little bit jarring here in the middle of London. I definitely had not expected that. "How are you?"

"I am good, Cleo, thank you."

"And what can I do for you today? I know better than to ask if you need some ink of your own done. Maybe for your friend here?" Cleo asked, looking over at me.

"Unfortunately, we do not have the time today. Today, we come looking only for information."

"Well, I have a lot of that as well," Cleo said with a wink at me. I smiled back at her. Cleo obviously had a lot of energy, and her happy personality was contagious. "Come, have a seat at the table and let me know what it is that I can do for the two of you."

She motioned for us to sit on the long bench and Cassie and I did so. I looked around, wondering where the actual tattooing took place, then realized it had to be behind the closed black door.

"I believe this is some of your work," Violet said, getting straight into it. She handed Cleo her phone, and the American woman nodded slowly a moment later.

"Yes, this is mine," Cleo replied. "I must have done this about a year ago?"

"What can you tell me about the customer who ordered it?" Violet asked.

Cleo frowned. "Wow, now you're asking for a lot. I think I vaguely remember the man who got this. He's not a regular; he walked in, saw the design on the wall, and told me he wanted it."

"Was he homeless?"

"No, but I have a feeling he wasn't exactly flush with cash," Cleo said slowly, trying to remember what she could about the man. "His credit card was declined when he went to pay, and he left me his driver's license while he went to an ATM to get some cash."

"You wouldn't have happened to have taken a photocopy of that driver's license, would you?" I asked, and Cleo's face lit up.

"You know, I think I might have. Let me into the back and find the man's file for you."

"This could be just the stroke of luck we were after," I said to Violet while we waited for Cleo to return.

"I hope so," Violet replied. "Cleopatra Blake is an absolutely remarkable woman, and it would not surprise me to learn that she had kept important information about her client."

"Blake... the name of the shop?"

"Yes," Violet nodded. "Cleopatra is related to William Blake, the author of the poem 'The Tyger', and that is from where she got the name of the parlor."

"And Cleopatra?" I said, raising my eyebrows.

"Perhaps her father was exceptionally arrogant," Violet said with a smile. "Seeing as the name derives from the Greek for 'loves her father'."

I laughed just as Cleo made her way back into the room, holding a manila folder happily over her head.

"Here you go, I found it!"

The two of us pored over the files as Cleo opened them up and handed them over. There was a picture of the original drawing, photos of the finished tattoo, with the typical red scarring that accompanied new ink, and a few scribbled notes, along with a photocopy of a drivers' license that Violet immediately grabbed.

"Where did he live?" I asked, peering over at the photocopy myself. The picture was definitely that of our murder victim. We finally had a name: Joseph Fenman.

"The address listed is one at Golden Lane Estate, a council estate on the outskirts of the city," Violet replied as she jotted down the address. "Hopefully, there is someone there who can help us to determine the man's identity."

After thanking Cleo for her time, and her telling us we should really consider getting tattoos in the future, Violet and I left, heading to our next stop: Golden Lane Estate.

CHAPTER 7

"*W*hy don't you want to get a tattoo?" I asked Violet as we sat in a cab taking us straight to our next stop.

"It is simply prudence. A tattoo, a permanent mark, makes you more identifiable. If you are ever required to conceal your identity, a tattoo makes that more difficult. I keep my body as mark-free as possible for when I am required to mask who I am."

"You know, sometimes you say things that make me think you're not always on the right side of the law," I said.

"Yes, that is correct. In my line of work, laws occasionally require breaking in order to solve a larger crime. You have accompanied me in such times. Tell me, if we were to get caught on camera sneaking into a suspect's home, would the presence of a tattoo be an advantage, or a hindrance?"

"Got it," I said, shaking my head slightly. Violet was completely insane sometimes, but at the same time, I could see her point. It was true that I had never committed so many felonies as I had since moving to England, in the sense that before moving here my running total had been exactly zero.

Now I was probably making my way towards double digits.

"Something as permanent as a tattoo requires long-term thinking."

"What would you get as a tattoo if you were to get one?" I asked, leaning back in the seat.

"I do not know. I have never thought about it, since I have never considered getting one."

"You have the worst imagination of anyone I have ever met."

"Why should one have the need for imagination when there is so much real wonder in the world?"

Wow. That was a surprisingly poignant response.

"I guess, but isn't our imagination the thing that sets us apart? Anyway, I don't really know what I would get if I were to get a tattoo. I like the idea of something symbolic, something that means a lot to me."

"Such as?"

"I don't know. Maybe a caduceus?" I replied, refer-encing the symbol of the staff with two serpents that represented medicine these days.

"Now that is telling," Violet replied with a small

smile. "Anyway, there is no time for you to continue imagining that which does not exist; we have arrived."

The taxi pulled up to the curb and the two of us got out, with Violet paying the driver while I looked around. We were surrounded by plain-looking brick buildings of varying heights, with most of them being around three to five stories tall, but with a couple that stood significantly taller. The buildings all had a real Soviet-style, built in the sixties look to them.

Violet checked her phone for the exact address, then pointed ahead to one of the low-rise buildings straight ahead. As we approached the door, someone was just leaving, so we didn't need to try and get someone to buzz us in.

I reached forward and grabbed the door before it closed, and the two of us made our way to the first floor apartment listed on the address. Violet knocked, and a couple of moments later, the door opened.

"Yes?" a woman answered. She was short, and thin. Incredibly thin. Her short, black hair was plastered against her head, and she looked like she hadn't slept in a few days.

"Hello, my name is Violet Despuis, and I am looking for a man who may have lived here in the past. Do you know a Joseph Fenman?" Violet asked. As soon as she said his name, the woman's eyes widened.

"Something's happened to him, hasn't it?"

"Why do you say that?" Violet asked.

"He was supposed to come by last night. He comes by here once every few weeks, to get a feed and have a shower. He's my brother, you see."

"Ah," I nodded. Now that she mentioned it, I could see the resemblance. They both had the same light brown, deep-set eyes.

"Has something happened to him?"

"We should step inside, perhaps," Violet said, and the woman burst into tears.

"I'm sorry to tell you, but your brother was found murdered this afternoon," I said softly. The tears turned into sobs, and the woman turned and entered her apartment. Violet and I shared a look, then slipped in after her.

"I'm so sorry," I said softly, while Violet made her way to the kitchen straight away and put some water in an electric kettle. I had now been in England for long enough that I knew she was making this woman a cup of tea. That seemed to be what people did whenever literally anything happened in this country. Stressful day at work? Cup of tea. Found out about the death of a loved one? Cup of tea. Won an Olympic gold medal? Cup of tea. It was just what was done.

I led the woman towards a ratty old couch and helped her sit down on it as she buried her head in her hands. Violet came by a moment later with the tea and the woman took it gratefully.

"What happened?" she finally asked, her voice hoarse.

"We don't know yet," Violet replied quietly. "You may have heard about the body found at King's cross this afternoon?"

"That was him? Oh, Joey," the woman cried. "Who on earth could have possibly done this to my poor brother?"

"I was hoping you would be able to help us figure that out," Violet said. "I am working with the police to try and find your brother's killer."

"Ask away," the woman said. "I'll do whatever I can to help you find the monster that did this to my baby brother."

"First of all, can I have your name?"

"Alyssa. Alyssa Fenman."

"Thank you, Alyssa. And your brother, he was homeless, correct?"

"He was," Alyssa confirmed. "He had always had a lot of trouble in his life. We both did, really. Joey was never able to hold down a job for that long, not since he came back from Iraq. He had PTSD, from the war, and it was like no matter how hard anyone tried, he just wouldn't get help. I tried to get him to live here with me, even though it's small, but we could have managed. Joey preferred the streets, though. Still, he came by from time to time to have a shower or for a hot meal if he really couldn't find anything. He used this place as his address for official documents. I tried to take care of him as best I could; I promised mum that I would before she died. Oh, I'm so glad she's not here to see this day."

Alyssa broke into sobs once more, and Violet and I waited a moment for them to abate before continuing with the questions.

"Do you know where your brother was last night?" I asked.

"He was supposed to be here," Alyssa replied. "He texted me. I made sure he had a phone so he could always get in touch with me if he needed to. He told me he was going to come by, but he never did. I don't know what his other plans were."

"When was the last time you saw your brother?" Violet asked.

"Just yesterday, but in the morning. I tripped, falling down a set of stairs at Baker Street station on my way back from work and hurt my wrist. I texted Joey, and he insisted on taking me to the hospital himself. He got me to A&E and waited with me while the doctor sent me for X-rays. It's not broken, just sprained. But that was the kind of person he was. Joey might have had some issues, but he was a good person. He didn't deserve this."

"How did he seem?" Violet asked. "That day you saw him, was there anything different about him?"

"No. No, I would have noticed if there was. I'm telling you, there was nothing the matter with him then."

"Alright," Violet said softly. "Do you know where he preferred to spend his time when he wasn't here?"

"He liked Regent's Park. I know he spent most of his days there. I don't know where he slept most of the time."

"Do you know if he had any friends?" I asked, and Alyssa shook her head.

"I'm afraid I have no idea. Joey didn't like to talk about his life with me. He always insisted on talking about me, instead. He always told me he was so proud of me."

"Alright, thank you, Alyssa," Violet told the woman. "We really appreciate it."

Alyssa nodded glumly. "What can I do about his body?"

"I will have someone contact you," Violet replied. "Can I get your phone number? And while I am at it, could you get me your brother's phone number as well?"

"Sure," Alyssa said, getting up off the couch and finding an old scrap of paper onto which she jotted a couple of numbers, handing them over to Violet.

"Please find the person who did this," she implored. "I know my brother didn't live a normal life, but he was a good person. He served this country. And he didn't deserve to die."

Violet nodded. "I will do everything I can to find your brother's killer."

As we left, I couldn't help but feel for the poor woman in there whose life had just been ripped apart. There had been no pictures of a boyfriend, no sign of a child, or any other sort of indication that Alyssa was close to anyone else. I had a feeling Joey had been all she had in this life.

I swore that I would do my best – whatever little I could offer – to help get justice for the poor woman.

CHAPTER 8

"*L*et me guess – the next step is to trace the phone number?" I asked, and Violet nodded.

"Yes. I will send this number to DCI Williams and have him send us all of the information."

"Is DCI Williams on this case?"

"No, but I prefer him to DCI Kilmer, who is a pompous git at best."

I smiled to myself as we hailed another cab and headed home.

"Well, I'll leave you to it, because unlike you, us mere mortals do require sleep."

"I will come and get you in the morning when I know what our next step is to be."

I really hoped it was going to take Violet eight hours to get another lead, but somehow I doubted a full night's sleep was in my future.

~

*S*ure enough, it was five in the morning when my phone began to ring. I grumbled and simply pressed the button on the side to mute the sound, but when it rang again immediately afterwards, I knew it was Violet. And I knew she wasn't going to let up, either. No matter what, I wasn't going to be getting any more sleep tonight. And as the events of the previous day flooded back to me, I realized I didn't really want to, either.

"Did you find out about the phone?" I asked.

"Yes," Violet replied. "DCI Williams was good enough to wake up a judge, and then find an employee at the phone company who was willing and able to get us what we wanted in the middle of the night."

"It's still the middle of the night."

"It absolutely is not. Now, come over here, and we will have breakfast before making our way to the hospital where Alyssa was seen yesterday, then to Regent's Park, which was the last place where our victim used his phone before being killed."

"Only if you promise this breakfast doesn't involve almond milk."

Just as the sun was rising over London, Violet and I were in a cab making our way over to University College Hospital. It was only two stops on the underground between Baker Street station and the hospital, so it made sense that it would have been where Alyssa had gone.

The two of us made our way to the accident and emergency ward, where we explained to a nurse that we needed to speak with the doctor who saw Alyssa Fenman the day before.

"I'm afraid that due to confidentiality laws, I'm unable to comment about anything regarding the woman's care," the nurse replied.

"We do not care about Alyssa or her wrist injury," Violet said. "You can call her for permission if you'd like. We simply need to speak to the doctor and any nurses who may have dealt with her to determine if anyone overheard something that might give us a clue as to who killed her brother."

The nurse looked from side to side for a minute, as if trying to decide what to do. I could tell she was on the edge, so I leaned forward.

"You know that body found at King's cross yesterday? That was Alyssa Fenman's brother. And we don't think he's the first victim. If you help us, you could be helping us find a serial killer."

At those words the nurse's eyes widened and she got up, motioning for us to wait for a moment as she got another nurse to take over the admissions desk. The nurse came out from behind the reception area and Violet and I followed her outside where she sat on a concrete wall, then sighed.

"As long as you don't ask me anything medically

relevant to Alyssa Fenman, I suppose I can answer your questions," the nurse said. "I saw her when she came in with her brother."

"Did you notice anything in particular about him?" Violet asked.

"He seemed to be rather jumpy," the nurse replied. "He didn't like the beeping of the heart rate monitor when I checked her pulse, and I have a feeling that he would have benefited from seeing a counselor."

That fit in with what Alyssa told us; his reaction to the beeps might have been because of his PTSD.

"Did you hear him speak to anybody, or use his phone, or mention what he was going to be doing later that day?" Violet asked, but the nurse only shook her head.

"Sorry. He didn't mention anything of the sort. He was all about his sister, doting on her. I don't think he mentioned himself even once."

"All right, thank you. Could you tell us which doctor saw her?"

"I guess so. If it will help find a killer. Speak with doctor King. He should be here now; his shift started two hours ago. I'll buzz you into the A&E wing, and if you wait by the nursing station he'll show up there eventually. He's the one with a parrot tattoo on his arm."

"Thank you," Violet said.

"Was it really her brother who was the victim of that murder yesterday?"

"It was," I replied sadly. The nurse shook her head.

"I hope you find the psycho who did that." And with that, she strode back into the hospital, with Violet and my following after her. She buzzed us through as she had promised, and Violet and I made our way to see Doctor King in the hopes that he might be able to shed some light for us.

We found him a couple of minutes later, and he looked exactly like the kind of kid that I absolutely hated back in medical school.

With brushed back blonde hair, a Jay Leno chin, blue eyes and a sneer that gave him the impression of looking down on everybody he saw, I had to admit my first impression of Doctor King was not the best one. He reminded me of the private school kids that came into medical school thinking they were the hottest thing around, driving Mercedes cars while the rest of us took the bus. It wasn't that I resented them for being rich, it was that I resented them for being rude about it. And sure enough, on his right bicep was a picture of a grey and pink parrot of some kind, just as the nurse had said.

However, as soon as he spoke, I felt a little bit bad for rushing to judgment.

"Violet Despuis, you're that famous detective that I've read about in the papers," he said, shaking her hand when she introduced herself. "I'm glad to see that you're working on this King's Cross case. It's a horrid business. And who might you be?"

"Cassie Coburn," I said, and Doctor King extended a hand to me as well. "I work with Violet in a consulting capacity."

That was my new fancy way of saying I followed her around, complained about her eating habits, and occasionally managed to supply some important medical information.

"Well, obviously I'll do anything I can to help. What do you want to know?"

"Did you notice anything about Alyssa's brother?" Violet asked, mirroring the same question she had asked the nurse a few minutes earlier.

"Well, apart from the obvious that the man had some mental issues," Doctor King said. "I'm no psychologist, but it wouldn't surprise me to learn that he was suffering from posttraumatic stress."

"That is correct," Violet nodded. "His sister confirmed that for us."

"Right. Well, I'm afraid I didn't notice anything else that caught my attention."

"Did he mention any plans he had for later on that day?"

"You know, now that you mention it, I think he did say something about meeting a friend in the park before going back to his sister's that afternoon."

"He spent most of his time in Regent's Park. Did you catch the friend's name by any chance?"

"I'm afraid not," Doctor King said, shaking his head. "Either he didn't mention it, or I can't remember. But he was definitely going to meet a friend. That's a nice place for someone in his situation to spend his time, the view overlooking the park is excellent. But I'm afraid I can't be more helpful."

"All right, thank you *docteur*."

"I'm sorry I couldn't be of more assistance. Do you have a card? If I think of anything else, I'd like to call you."

Violet pulled a card from her wallet and handed it over to the doctor, who saluted her with it the way that men do before tucking it into the pocket of his lab coat.

As we left the hospital, I turned to Violet. "Well, at least now we know what we're looking for in Regent Park."

CHAPTER 9

*L*uckily for us, Regent's Park was only a couple of minutes' walk from the hospital, so there was no need to take a taxi and instead Violet and I enjoyed the brisk walk, on a morning that was a little bit warmer than the previous few had been.

"Wait here one moment," Violet told me just before we entered the park, and she entered a little bakery and came back a few moments later with a bag full of goodies.

Regent's Park reminded me a lot of my personal favorite park in London, Hyde Park. Huge, wide paths were lined on either side with giant trees that had all lost their leaves at this point in the year. Hedges and smaller bushes dotted the landscape, as Londoners of all types enjoyed the atmosphere of the green space. There were mothers with their children being pushed along in strollers, business people on the phone who use the park as a shortcut to get where they wanted to be, tourists taking pictures of everything they could see, and dogs being taken for a walk, stopping to sniff every few meters.

Regent's Park was pretty big, even by London standards. I didn't really know where to go, and obviously, neither did Violet. We ended up walking rather aimlessly along the paths, looking around, until finally Violet pointed at a man sitting under one of the large trees off to the side, on the grass. He was surrounded by an army duffel bag full of stuff, and was obviously homeless. Maybe he knew Joseph Fenman.

"Excuse me, sir," Violet asked, making her way over to the man. He grunted at her and held his bag closer to him. "I'm wondering if you know a Joseph, or Joey Fenman?"

Realizing Violet wasn't there to accost him, the man relaxed a bit, then took a croissant from the bag Violet offered him. "Joey? Yeah, I know him. He's not around today, though."

"He was killed yesterday afternoon," Violet replied, and the man let out a low whistle.

"No kidding? Well, rest in peace, my man."

"Did you know him well?"

"Sure. As well as I know anyone around here."

"He was supposed to meet someone here yesterday afternoon. Any idea who that was?"

"News to me. If you head out towards the zoo,

though, there's a man round that way named Pete. He might know. He and Joey were close."

"Thank you," Violet replied. "As I do not know yet why Joey was killed, you may want to take some extra precautions with your safety. "It is possible that whoever killed your friend is targeting the homeless."

"Thanks for the warning, but I can take care of myself," the man replied.

"So could Joey," Violet replied. "Please, be careful."

"Will do. Thanks for the food," the man replied, and Violet and I made our way back towards the path, heading north to the London Zoo.

We found Peter lying on a bench, watching the clouds.

"Peter?" I asked when we saw him, and he sat up. Violet offered him the bag of croissants, and he eagerly took one.

"What can I do for two gorgeous young ladies this morning?"

"We heard you were supposed to meet with Joey Fenman yesterday afternoon," Violet replied.

"Sure. Joey said he found a lady who worked at a restaurant a ways away who was always willing to give us some extra food at the end of the night. We were going to see her before they shut, but he never showed."

"You didn't see him at all yesterday?" I asked.

"Well, I saw him in the morning. Then his sister called on that fancy phone of his, and he told me he had to go, and he'd meet me back here later. I stayed out here until late, but he never came back."

I frowned. So Peter was the man Joey had planned on meeting. That jived with what Doctor King had told us at the hospital. And yet, he had never made it here. I assumed Peter was telling the truth; he was too tall to be the man in the video we had seen at the hotel, and his hair was far too long. There was no way he could be the killer, so what reason did he have to lie?

"Do you have any idea why Joey did not come to meet you?"

"None at all. Just know he wasn't here when he was supposed to be."

"Alright, thank you," Violet said, and as we left the park, she was quiet.

"We're out of leads, aren't we?" I asked.

"There are always more leads we can follow. Sometime between the hospital and the park, Joseph Fenman disappeared. It is a question of finding out why. I will leave you to go home, and I will endeavor to discover more information that may be useful.

"And what happens if you don't find anything new?"

"Then, with this being a serial killer, we wait until he strikes again. He will strike again, and when he does, he will leave more evidence in his wake. We can only hope that he decides to do it publicly once more."

"Great," I said. "Well, I hope we manage to find him before then."

"As do I," Violet replied. "However, it is not

promising that we are this low on evidence this early in an investigation."

Leaving me with that thought, I headed off and tried to decide what I was going to do. I didn't really want to go home; all I would do there was think about the case and try to ignore the pile of admission papers on my desk.

Normally, I would call Jake, and see if he wanted to spend some time with me, but with the pathology report needing to be done as quickly as possible, I had a sneaking suspicion that Jake wasn't going to be able to get away for a while to have lunch with me. Besides, at this point, when he got off from work I suspected his number one priority would be getting some sleep.

Instead, I texted the one person that I knew would be more excited than anybody else about a potential serial killer: my best friend Brianne.

While she was a medical student, Brianne was definitely obsessed with crime and murder. She thought what Violet did as a job was the coolest thing ever, and was always eager to hear about her new cases. I asked her about it once, and Brianne told me that Violet's stories were better than any true crime podcast could ever be.

I sent her a text and found out she was at work. Brianne paid for her education in part by working at Chipotle on Baker Street, and I was always happy to stop by and have a delicious burrito bowl that tasted exactly like home. Chipotle had gotten me through quite a few late exam nights in my day.

I made my way back to the entrance of Regent's Park where we had come in, which was closest to Baker Street, and headed down to Brianne. She was working the counter, and as soon as she saw me she gave me a smile as I got into line.

"The usual?" she asked me, and I nodded.

"Yes, please. When's your break?"

"Whenever I want, really. I'll probably take it after this lunch rush is over," Brianne replied. "If you take about twenty minutes to eat that food, that should be about long enough."

"Cool," I replied, taking my food and sitting at one of the tables as I waited for Brianne's break to start. Sure enough, when the line died down about twenty minutes later, she made her way over to me, a burrito bowl in hand.

"I could eat four of these after today," Brianne commented, shoving a giant forkful into her mouth. "This day has been crazy. I don't know if it's a full moon or what, but everyone wants Mexican food today, and everyone is definitely not on their best behavior. I had one man complain that there were too many spices in the rice – *the rice!* – and a lady who asked if it was possible to make her burrito look 'less ethnic.'"

"I didn't know it was possible to live in London and

dislike food from other cultures," I laughed. "I swear, this place makes San Francisco look monochromatic."

"I know, right? It was a problematic comment on a whole bunch of levels. But anyway, enough about me. Are you really working with Violet on that King's Cross murder?"

"How do you know about that?"

"It was in the paper this morning. Violet Despuis, famous detective, helps police to solve brazen daylight murder."

"Well, it's no surprise the papers have it wrong as usual, the victim wasn't killed during the day. He was actually killed the night before, his body was moved onto the roof of the train station, and then just dropped through the glass panels before rush hour started."

"That's insane," Brianne replied through a mouthful of rice and chicken. "But so it's true, Violet is working on it, and you're helping her?"

I nodded. "Definitely. I mean, I'm not sure how much I'm helping at all. I'm basically just following her around and seeing what happens, but it is interesting."

"Do you know who did it yet?"

I shook my head. "No, and we're actually out of leads. Violet's out looking to see if she can figure out what happened to the victim after he left the hospital, where he was with his sister who sprained her wrist, but if not, then I think all we can do is wait for the killer to strike again."

"So you think it's a serial killer," Brianne said, her mouth dropping open.

"That's what Violet thinks, anyway. I think she's right, I don't think it's the first time that this person has killed someone. He's too good at it. I think I know Violet well enough by now that I can say that no first time killer would manage to fool her for this long."

"Definitely. If I've learned anything from watching a lot of TV, it's that serial killers often require validation. He's probably killed a number of people before, but the police have never linked them together, or come even close to figuring out who he is. He's probably gotten frustrated, and decided to commit this crime for the attention. By dropping the body in the middle of the busiest train station in London right before rush hour, he guarantees that the police are going to have to pay attention to him now."

"But doesn't that increase the risk of him getting caught? If he likes killing so much, why doesn't he just keep doing it without drawing attention to himself?"

"Because the serial killer in this situation needs to feel smarter than the police. He's taunting them. It's exactly the same as the Zodiac Killer back in your neck of the woods."

I nodded slowly. That made sense, for sure. "Okay, so under your theory my guess is that when he kills again, he's going to make it a public spectacle once more?"

"That's right," Brianne nodded. "I'd be willing to bet almost anything on it."

"Well, personally, I'm hoping that Violet manages to get a lead from whatever she's doing and that we'll be able to catch the killer before he strikes again."

"I must say, if I was a serial killer, I definitely would not want to be working out of the same area as Violet Despuis," Brianne said.

"Well, maybe that's why you're not a serial killer," I laughed.

"Not that you know, anyway," Brianne said with a wink.

I laughed. Brianne was always fun, and it was nice to talk things over with her. She always had an interesting perspective on the crimes that Violet and I were trying to solve. And in this case, I had a sneaking suspicion that she was right about the serial killer. What she had said made sense. Maybe he was now trying to get the attention of the police, and trying to prove that he was smarter than them by not being caught.

He had to be especially arrogant to think that he was smarter than Violet, though. My money was definitely on her.

CHAPTER 10

After half an hour, Brianne had to go back to work, and I wandered around somewhat aimlessly. Christmas was just a few days away, and while I had found something for Jake ages ago – he had mentioned that he needed a new watch in passing, so I bought him a nice one – I had absolutely no idea what to buy Violet. What did you get a woman who seemingly had all the money in the world, and at the same time, apparently no interest in material things? I made my way back to my apartment after two hours, none the wiser in terms of a gift. Normally, for someone who had everything, I would bake cookies. But Violet would just complain about the fat and sugar content, and I refused to make healthy cookies as a gift out of principle. So, I was just going to have to keep hunting for a gift and hope I came up with an idea in time.

Biscuit whined at the door pretty quickly, and I

decided to take him out for a walk, thinking about the case as we made our way up to Hyde Park, ignoring the looks from people who had obviously never seen a cat happily being walked on a leash before.

Biscuit's former owner, a murder victim from the first case that I had worked with Violet, had obviously taught him how to walk nicely on the leash, since he was already trained by the time I had adopted him. I had never really thought about walking a cat before, but he seemed to enjoy it so much I just couldn't stop doing it for him.

As much as I thought about things though, I couldn't quite piece the case together. Who had killed Joseph Fenman? Why? Was it just because he was there? The homeless were vulnerable in many ways, and often found themselves the victims of random attacks because of it. Was this why Joseph had been targeted?

I just didn't have the answers right now.

Instead, my mind turned to the looming deadline to enroll in medical school here. It was interesting how hard of a decision it was, when for so long, becoming a doctor was all I had ever wanted in life. Now, however, I just wasn't sure. I had always wanted to be a surgeon. I enjoyed working with my hands, and I liked the idea of stitching people up. That was impossible now, so if I was going to become a doctor, I was going to have to find a new specialty.

That was easier said than done. So should I do it

at all? Would I be happy being a doctor if I wasn't a surgeon? And was it worth it to try? Was it fair to everyone else for whom this was a dream job to take a spot for something I didn't really want to do? Would I be happy being a doctor for the rest of my life in a specialty I didn't really want to do, or would I go to work every morning blaming the driver who hit me in the parking lot and changed my life forever?

They were all important questions, and they were all questions that I couldn't answer just yet. And at the same time, I had other questions. What was I going to do if I didn't become a doctor? I was exceedingly lucky that thanks to an insurance payout I had plenty of money, and no need to make a decision immediately. But a decision would have to be made. I certainly couldn't live my life floating along, just following Violet as she solved crimes and being a complete drain on society. I wanted to be more than that. I wanted my life to mean something. I wanted to help people. That was why I had wanted to become a doctor in the first place, because I wanted to help people. I wasn't going to be the type of person who sat around doing nothing forever.

But I also didn't want whatever I eventually did to make me miserable.

I sighed as Biscuit and I headed back home. There were no easy answers to the questions that I had, and I certainly wasn't going to figure them out now. Maybe I should just defer my admission for another semester. After all, I could start my new class in June.

But then, when did it end? Would I continue deferring forever? No, I couldn't keep doing this. I had to make a decision, and I had to do it soon. I had a deadline, and I was going to meet it.

I just had absolutely no idea what I was going to do yet.

~

I hadn't really expected to hear from Violet that afternoon, and sure enough, I didn't. I figured that her hunt for more evidence had not been exactly fruitful. The next morning, however, my phone buzzed from a text.

There is another body. Meet me outside.

My heart sunk in my chest at the words. I had really hoped that we would find the killer before he struck again, but it appeared that we were going to have no such luck.

I grabbed my things, gave Biscuit a quick pat on the head, then made my way out to the street where Violet was already waiting. A moment later, an unmarked police car pulled up, and DCI Kilmer motioned for the two of us to get in.

"Where is the body this time?" Violet asked as soon as her butt hit the seat.

"The Sherlock Holmes Museum."

"Well, there's a little bit of irony," I muttered as the car sped away from the curb, taking us to the new crime scene.

The Sherlock Holmes museum, on Baker Street, wasn't actually that far from the Chipotle where Brianne worked. I sent her a text, letting her know that if she was around, there was a lot of murder-related excitement right here.

Unfortunately, there was also chaos. Baker Street wasn't in and of itself a main thoroughfare of London, but it was close enough to at least a couple of main streets that the fact that it was the current home to the media circus, it was leading to, yet again, ridiculous traffic problems.

I had a feeling the media was about to change tactics: no serial killer could be allowed to go unchecked if the discovery of his victims led to such traffic jams.

It took a few minutes, but thanks to the flashing lights on the car and tactical use of the sirens to go with it, the car carrying DCI Kilmer, Violet, and I eventually pulled up to one of the most famous pop-culture related museums in the world.

The Sherlock Holmes museum was housed in a red-brick building, with the ground floor being painted white. Next door was Hudson's restaurant, with a Beatles' memorabilia shop on the other side. The fancy red velvet barrier ropes on bronze posts had been replaced with yellow crime scene tape, and the fancy late-

1800s-style cop "guarding" the front door had been replaced with modern constables. With a flash of his badge at the front door, the three of us were led through, while reporters hurled questions at us – ok, at DCI Kilmer and at Violet, not at me – that were promptly ignored.

"Miss Despuis, is it true the Metropolitan police have put you in charge of this case?"

"Do the police have any leads?"

"Is this related to the killing at King's Cross yesterday?"

As soon as the door was shut behind us, the questions were cut off, and we made our way upstairs.

"The body was found first thing this morning, as soon as the first staff arrived," DCI Kilmer explained as we climbed a narrow staircase. "They called us straight away, and it was pretty obvious what killed her."

Sure enough, right around the woman's neck was a thick, purple bruise. I was no pathologist, but it wasn't a stretch to assume she had been strangled as well.

Much like the other victim, this woman had obviously been dressed up as well. However, rather than wearing a suit, this woman was dressed exactly like a woman from the late 1800s, complete with corset, a long, blue dress and even a fancy hat. Yes, it was obvious that whoever was killing the people was putting on a show.

The woman was spread across a long settee, beige in color, right underneath the spot in the wall where the letters 'VR' – Victoria Regina – meaning 'Queen

Victoria' in Latin, had been shot into the deep red patterned wallpaper. Two sconce lamps on either side shone dramatic light onto the victim.

There was not a doubt in my mind that this was all done on purpose. This crime scene had been staged almost perfectly, and it was like the killer was taunting the police and Violet to be just as good as Sherlock Holmes.

I had to admit, despite the fact that it was horrifying and incredibly creepy, there was something very artistic about the way the body had been set up. Looking around at the faces of the police officers, I could tell that it had had the desired effect. They were worried; the brash confidence that they were going to be able to solve this case no matter what just wasn't there. Instead, their faces read the fear of being blasted in the media. The fear of another body appearing in a couple of days. The fear of being labeled failures, of not being able to find the serial killer.

Violet, on the other hand, looked exactly like she did at any other crime scene. She examined the body, being careful not to move anything, and was busy looking in the victim's mouth when Jake walked in.

"As much as I'm sure you think you can do my job for me, I am a pretty good pathologist," he said to Violet as he strode confidently towards the body and opened his bowler bag, pulling out the equipment he was going to need to do his on the spot examination. He looked up and flashed a smile at me, which I returned immediately. It was like every time Jake entered the room I was in, the temperature rose a few degrees, and my heart swelled with pleasure.

"Perhaps if you had appeared sooner, I would not have had to begin a physical examination myself," Violet replied, and Jake shot her a look that somehow only he could get away with. I would not have envied any police officers who gave her the same look.

"I guess I'm just not as important as you; I only found out about this body fifteen minutes ago. Now, if you'll excuse me, feel free to look around and look for more clues while I get started on this. I assume you want the time of death first?"

"Yes," Violet replied. "Although judging by rigor mortis I believe she was killed later than the last victim; perhaps a little bit after midnight."

"What do you even need me here for?" Jake joked as he got to work.

Violet stepped away from the body and began looking around the rest of the room. It was small and cramped; there were at least ten police officers in the room, not to mention all of the equipment, and I was starting to feel a little bit claustrophobic.

"All right," Violet announced a moment later in a loud voice. "Everybody out!"

It appeared I wasn't the only one annoyed by the people in the room. A low murmur of dissent broke out, and Violet clapped her hands. "I mean it. None of you are doing anything useful, you are all just here to gawk at the body. There are too many people, you are contaminating my crime scene, get out."

"Your crime scene? You're not even with the police," a voice called out from somewhere in the room.

"Neither will you be if you do not get out right now."

DCI Kilmer eventually nodded to the group of officers. "Do as she asks. I want you to start canvassing the neighborhood; see if anybody saw anything suspicious happening out here, especially around midnight."

This time, while there was some unhappy grumbling, the officers knew better than to disobey a superior, and they stalked out of the room unhappily, leaving only Violet, Jake, DCI Kilmer and myself. It was definitely a much more manageable number of people.

"Good, now maybe I can hear myself think," Violet muttered.

For everyone's sake, I hoped so.

*a*s Jake worked on the body, Violet began inspecting the room, while DCI Kilmer muttered something about working on the canvas and left quickly. I made my way towards the window, looking out onto Baker Street where reporters and curious bystanders were huddled against the blue and white police tape, trying desperately and in vain to get a look at something a little bit exciting to do with the murder.

I couldn't help but smile when I spotted Brianne walking towards the group, though she didn't stay long. I knew she was curious, but she also wasn't morbid.

Eventually, I stepped away from the window and began looking around the room myself. It reminded me a lot of my grandmother's house, with little knick-knacks and items absolutely everywhere. Above the door that led into the next room was an old rifle and a spear, the wall was covered in paintings and some sort of animal skull. Two bookshelves on either side of the mantle were filled with both books and other knick-knacks, a small writing desk featured a violin and various smoking paraphernalia. On the mantle was an old-style clock, a couple of statues, and some candles and fancy holders. A small, round table in front featured a classic deerstalker hat Sherlock Holmes is so known for, a magnifying glass, and in a homage to Doctor Watson, a stethoscope and a very primitive pacemaker. A chair in the corner was covered with books about all sorts of topics, and a table against the window next to the body was set as if Holmes and Watson were getting ready for morning tea.

I couldn't see how any of this had anything to do with the murder.

"Was there any identification on the body?" I asked nobody in particular, and Violet answered.

"There will not have been," she said. "The killer is far too careful for that. However, there are other ways to identify a person than by cards carried on their body."

"So you know who this is, then."

"I do not know her name, however, I do believe I know where we can find out who she is. Her skin has the faint aroma of chlorine if sniffed carefully, the way someone who spends a large portion of their time in a pool would smell."

"Well, forgive me for not having sniffed the murder victim's skin at close range," I said with a smile, and Violet shook her head.

"It is important when investigating a murder that not a single step is skipped. If it wasn't for that smell, it would have been far more difficult to determine this woman's identity. On top of the faint smell, if you look closely at her hairline a number of the hairs right at the front of her scalp have been torn, which is common among swimmers who are constantly putting on bathing caps, which make it so easy to pull out a few hairs."

"Okay, so she spends a lot of time in a pool," I said. "There have to be a whole bunch of them in London."

"Yes, but look at her tan line."

"Her tan line?" I asked.

"Yes, pull up her dress and you will see what I mean," Violet said. I did as she asked and saw that halfway down the woman's thighs, sure enough, there was a pretty obvious tan line.

"Okay, so she has been out of the country recently, because I'm pretty sure there's literally nowhere in England where you can get a tan like this at this time of year, and absolutely nobody would go into a tanning booths with shorts on."

"Good," Violet said, and I scrunched my face, trying to figure out what my brain was trying to tell me.

"So we have a woman who spends a lot of her time in the pool, and who was swimming outside of the country recently." A link formed in my brain, and I made my way up to the woman's shoulder, where I checked to see what her tan mark on her arm looked like. It was just a normal tan, like she had been wearing a tank top or something. "The top of her suit was sleeveless, which means that it probably wasn't a wetsuit. Besides, if it was a wetsuit, she would have presumably been wearing it in open water and not in a pool, so she wouldn't have that chlorine smell anyway."

"*Excellent*, Cassie. Keep going."

"Since she was in a pool, given the shape of the tan line, it looks like one of those suits the swimmers wear at the Olympics. Was she a professional swimmer?"

"*Parfait*," Violet said with a smile and an enthusiastic clap of her hands. "You have figured it out perfectly."

"Great, so what we need to do now is find a list of professional swimmers in England who might have recently been overseas swimming."

"I am way ahead of you," Violet replied, holding up her phone. "At this time last week, there was a World Cup swimming event in Australia, which took place in an open air pool."

"And seeing as December is the middle of summer in Australia, it would've been very easy for the swimmers to get a tan from their suits while at the meet," I finished.

"That is correct," Violet replied. "Luckily, with it being such an important event in the world of swimming, I was able to Google a list of competitors, and found that there were four women from the UK competing. One of them, Marnie Phillips, looks exactly like our murder victim."

Violet handed me her phone, which was open on a Google search for Marnie Phillips, and sure enough, the woman whose smiling face wearing a full racing suit and a bathing cap, with swimming goggles hanging around her neck, was the same woman now lying dead in front of us.

"Poor woman," I muttered, shaking my head and handing the phone back to Violet. "I suppose the next step is to go find out where she lived?"

"Yes," Violet replied. "If you don't mind, could you go find DCI Kilmer and ask him to get an address for us?"

I nodded. "Sure thing."

"That sure is something," Jake said as he watched the two of us. "I can now tell you for sure that Violet was right; Marnie Phillips was killed sometime between midnight and two o'clock this morning. But somehow, that doesn't seem quite as impressive after just having seen you figure out who she was."

"Thanks," I grinned, giving Jake a quick wave as I made my way back down the stairs and out to the Street, where I found DCI Kilmer passing orders to a couple of uniformed officers.

"What do you have?" he asked as soon as he saw me.

"We need an address for Marnie Phillips," I replied.

"She's a swimmer at the World Cup level for England, and she is our murder victim."

DCI Kilmer let out a groan. "Great. That's just what we need; someone in the public eye who's a role model as our murder victim."

"Can you get me the information?"

"Yes. Of course. I'll get it upstairs to Violet in the next five minutes."

CHAPTER 12

*H*alf an hour later, Violet was finished inspecting the crime scene, and the two of us made our way to Marnie Phillips' address. She didn't live too far from Baker Street, just a couple of blocks away from Camden Town underground station, on the other side of the park from Baker Street.

Through her Googling, Violet had discovered that Marnie Phillips was married, and we were about to have to give her husband some very, very bad news.

Ringing the buzzer to be let in, a part of me really hoped there was going to be no answer. After all, if we couldn't find the husband, we couldn't tell him his wife was dead.

Unfortunately, I had no such luck. Ten, maybe fifteen seconds after ringing the buzzer at the bottom, a man's voice replied.

"Yes?"

"Mr. Phillips, my name is Violet Despuis and I'm working with the police. Could you let me and my associate up?"

"Of course," came his answer, and a moment later the front door buzzed, indicating that it was unlocked and ready for us to enter.

Climbing a narrow set of stairs, Violet and I quickly found ourselves in front of a plain door surrounded by cracking old pieces of wallpaper. It was obvious that this building had not been renovated in quite some time; I began to wonder if maybe these pieces of wallpaper had actually been there during the Blitz.

Violet knocked on the door, and a moment later it opened, revealing a tall, medium build man with a thin face, an aquiline nose, and blue eyes that had obviously been crying. He looked from Violet to me, his eyes moving quickly. This was obviously a man who was worried about something.

"Have you found her? Is she okay?" the man asked.

"Mr. Phillips, I'm sorry to have to tell you but Marnie's body was found this morning on Baker Street," Violet told him softly. "Please, let us come inside. You should sit down."

It was as though the man deflated right in front of us. He seemed to shrink by a few inches, and his shoulders slumped, his eyes now staring blankly at the ground. He opened the door wordlessly and let Violet and I in, then made his way to a stuffed chair in the living room and collapsed onto it.

"Is she really dead?" he finally managed to ask, and Violet nodded, making her way to the couch across from the chair and sitting down on it.

"We need to ask you some questions, is that all right?" she asked, receiving a nod in response.

"Yes."

"Do you know where Marnie was last night?"

"She went to the gym. She got back from Australia three days ago, and she was still suffering from jet lag. She was hoping that by doing a late-night work out she would be tired enough to go to sleep as soon as she came home, and get back onto a regular sleep schedule before starting her training sessions again tomorrow."

"Which gym did she attend?"

"The Gym at Bloomsbury," Phillips replied. "It's a twenty-four hour gym, which she liked because it allowed her to train whenever she wanted. She jogs there from here, which takes her fifteen minutes, which she considers to be the perfect warm-up. On the way back, she takes the tube, since she's usually too knackered to run back as well."

"Her Oyster card wouldn't happen to be here, would it?" Violet asked, but Mr. Phillips shook his head.

"No, she took it with her last night. She never came home. I stayed up, worried. She left at eleven, and when she wasn't back by one I started to wonder. I called her phone, and she should have answered, since she uses it to listen to music while she works out. But there was no answer. I texted, but again, nothing. I went out myself, I took her route to get down there, and when I got there someone let me in. But she wasn't there. That was when I called 999."

"They told you that they could not file an official missing person's report until she had been missing for longer?" Violet asked, and Mr. Phillips nodded.

"Yes, exactly that. I knew something was wrong and I spent the whole night wandering around, looking for her. You said she was at Baker Street?"

"That is correct," Violet said. "We believe she was the victim of a serial killer, who staged her body in the Sherlock Holmes Museum."

Mr. Phillips buried his face in his hands. "Oh, Marnie. I can't believe someone would do this to her. She was such a pure soul. Not a mean bone in her body. She wanted to be the best. She was going to be the best. She was going to compete at Tokyo, at her last Olympic Games, and then she was going to retire and we were going to have children."

"I'm so sorry," I said to him, my heart breaking for the man who had just lost the love of his life. I couldn't imagine what he was going through right now.

"You say it was a serial killer who did this. Do you know who it is yet?"

"I have an idea," Violet said. I wondered if she was lying to the man to make him feel better, but I had a sneaking suspicion she wasn't. That didn't sound like Violet at all. If she said she had an idea, then she did have an idea. "What did your wife do the rest of the time since she came back from Australia? Was there anything out of the ordinary that you can think of?"

"She just slept, mostly. I know she was up quite early yesterday, at maybe two in the morning, but that was the jetlag. She went back to bed around eight, and woke up again around noon. Yesterday afternoon she went out to get groceries, came back, and watched some TV before going to do her work out. There was really nothing out of the ordinary there, and she didn't seem like she was acting strangely at all."

"Had she mentioned anyone following her, or anything of the sort?"

"Nothing like that, no," Mr. Phillips said. "She had barely been out of the house since she got back. She had gone to the gym a couple of times, and she went to get those groceries, but that was about it. The rest of the time she mainly stayed here and slept or studied video of her technique on the computer."

Violet frowned slightly. I could see she wasn't happy with the answers Mr. Phillips was giving her, but I didn't know what she was thinking. I wasn't sure what she was looking for.

After asking a few more questions that also went nowhere, Violet eventually stood up.

"Thank you for your time," she told Mr. Phillips. "I'm very sorry for your loss. Members of the metropolitan police will likely be here later to ask you very similar questions to those I have just asked."

"Right," Mr. Phillips answered. "Please, do whatever you have to do to find the killer."

Violet nodded and the two of us headed back out into the street.

"What are you thinking? You obviously have a suspect in mind, so who is it?"

"I *had* a suspect in mind," Violet replied. "Unfortunately, Mr. Phillips answers did not eliminate him, but they also do not suit the pattern I had been expecting to see, either."

I nodded. "Are we going to go to the gym, seeing as that's the last place where Marnie was before she was killed?"

"We do not yet know that she even reached the gym," Violet corrected. "However, you are correct. We will go over there, we will see if Marnie was there, and we can hope that someone else who was there around the same time will have seen something."

The entrance to The Gym Bloomsbury was almost like entering a subway station. The exterior entrance was a ten foot by ten foot piece of glass, with stairs leading down into the actual gym area. When we finally made our way down and entered through some futuristic-looking round doors, a computer against the wall invited us to join, telling us it was "easy peasy".

The nearby wall was covered with biographies of all of the personal trainers, and three vending machines next to it sold water, sports drinks, and snacks. A fit-looking woman dressed in a polo shirt reading 'The Gym' sat at a desk nearby, on a bright blue stool.

"Hello," Violet said. "I am wondering if it would be possible to speak with the manager."

"Are you thinking about joining up?" the woman asked in a peppy voice. "I can definitely help you if you're having problems using the computer."

I hid a smile; Violet was better with computers than 99% of the people in this country.

"No, thank you. One of your clients was murdered after leaving here last night, and I would like to get some more information about her habits."

The blood drained from the woman's face. "Of course. Yes. Follow me, please."

Violet and I followed the woman past rows and rows of cardio machines, until we reached a closed door. The woman knocked, then unlocked it, leading us into a small office with a desk in the middle, covered in papers. Behind it sat a very muscular woman who must have competed in bodybuilding competitions in the past, if she didn't still do so.

"Yes, Jessica?"

"Elise, these two women say that someone from this gym was murdered after leaving yesterday. They have some questions they want to ask."

"Thank you, Jessica," the woman nodded, and Jessica closed the door behind us. "Are you with the police?"

"We are working with them," Violet said.

"Right. You're Violet Despuis. This is about that body at King's Cross, then?"

"Another body. This time at the Sherlock Holmes Museum," Violet answered, and the woman tutted.

"Such a shame. You say the victim worked out here?"

"That is correct. Marnie Philips."

"Oh, the swimmer. Yes, she's in here quite a bit. She's been killed, then?"

"Yes," I replied. "She was here last night."

"Let me check on that," Elise replied, her perfectly manicured fingers tapping away at the keyboard in front of her. She pressed the enter key with a flourish, and then nodded.

"Yes, it says here that Marnie entered the premises at 11:17 last night, and left at 12:47 this morning."

"Alright, so she did make it into the gym," I muttered.

"How does it work, here, late at night?" I asked. "Is there always staff around?"

"Not always," Elise replied. "We do have staff around during regular gym hours, but at night, for safety reasons, the front doors are locked, except to members. Every member has a PIN code that they use to access the gym. For safety reasons, there are CCTV cameras that cover every inch of the space, and there are emergency buttons that our clients can press if they ever feel unsafe."

"Is the gym busy at night, around when Marnie was here?" I asked.

"Certainly," Elise replied with a nod. "In fact, late at night, when other gyms are closed, are some of our busiest times. We have a lot of shift workers – everyone from security guards, to grocery store stockers, to doctors and nurses, to cab drivers and many others who don't work a typical 9-5 schedule, but still want to be able to access the gym when it suits them."

"So there would have been a number of people there when Marnie was working out?" Violet asked. "Are any of them here now, by chance?"

"Let me have a look, this will take a moment," Elise said, biting her bottom lip in concentration as she tapped away at the computer. "Okay, sure. There is one person here right now who was also here last night. Let me go grab him for you."

This was promising. Hopefully whoever this was had seen something that might help us figure out who the serial killer was.

Of course, I was also very aware that it was possible that whoever Marnie had run into who had led to her demise had met her well outside of the gym. I imagined that Violet already had it on her to do list to get CCTV footage for everywhere between the gym and the underground station.

Still, there was a chance it wasn't going to come to that. We were about to find out.

CHAPTER 13

*a*bout three or four minutes later, Elise came back into the room, followed by a guy who, as soon as I saw him, didn't surprise me at all that he had been here less than twelve hours earlier. The guy's biceps were about the size of my face, he could probably squat at least 400 pounds, but as he waved his face in the towel and threw on a hoodie while entering the room, he grinned at Violet and I before holding out a hand.

"I hear you're looking for someone who was here last night," he said. "That's me. I'm usually here twice a day, before and after work. Call me Johnny."

"What you do, out of curiosity, Johnny?" I asked.

"I work in the city, trading mainly on the ASX. Since I work out of Sydney's time zone, my hours make this the most convenient gym near my place."

Stockbroker. I had to admit, I had not expected

that. I thought for sure he was going to say security guard, construction worker, something like that. But hey, that was what I got for assuming things about people, wasn't it?

"You were here last night when this woman left," Violet said, holding her phone out to Johnny, who took it and squinted at the picture for a minute.

"Yeah, I was. I saw her last night. She was working legs. She's strong, too. I was using the weights that overlooked the entrance when she was leaving."

Violet leaned forward, her eyes gleaming. "Did you notice anything suspicious as she left? Did you notice anyone following her? Did anyone else leave the gym a minute or two after?"

Johnny thought for a second, then shook his head slowly.

"No, I don't think so. I don't think anyone left after her."

Elise tapped away at her keyboard for a minute, and then nodded. "Johnny is right. After Marnie left, the next person to leave the gym was twelve minutes later."

"There was something though," Johnny said thoughtfully. "As she was leaving, I'm pretty sure I heard her calling out to someone."

"Did you see who?" Violet asked quickly, but Johnny shook his head.

"No. Since the weights area is a bit elevated, you can't really see out all that far. Whoever it was wasn't close enough to the door for me to see. And it may not have been that. Maybe she just got on the phone, or something."

"Alright, thank you," Violet said, and Johnny nodded.

"Sure. Anything I can do to help. I hope you find who did this."

With that, Johnny got up from the chair and made his way back to the gym.

"Can I see the CCTV feeds from last night?" Violet asked.

"Sure," Elise replied, tapping away on the computer once more. After a minute or so, she turned the screen to Violet and handed her the mouse. "Here you go."

Violet immediately set the camera that focused on the stairs to full screen, and scrolled back to the previous night. Sure enough, at 12:48am, Marnie Philips came into view. She was with someone, a man. A gym bag was propped up over her shoulder. They stood in the corner, perfectly positioned so that the man's features couldn't be made out; his back was to the camera. After speaking for a moment, Marnie turned and continued back up the stairs, but the man stayed where he was. About thirty seconds later, he turned and followed Marnie back up the steps.

"Do you have any footage from outside?"

"Sorry," Elise said, shaking her head. "Is that... him?"

"We do not know," Violet said. "He is barely noticeable in this frame. I believe it may be the same man from the hotel, though."

Elise shuddered. "I can't believe it."

"Interestingly, she seemed to know the man," I muttered.

"That is because I would be willing to bet he is a member here," Violet replied, and Elise's face went white.

"Are you sure?"

"It is a reasonable assumption. If Marnie saw the man as she was leaving, that means that presumably he was at least partway down these stairs when she saw him."

"Right," I nodded.

"Our list of members is really quite long," Elise said apologetically. "And I'm afraid I can't simply give it to you. You would need a warrant."

"We can get one," Violet nodded, pulling out her phone and sending a text.

"Please do. I don't like knowing that one of our members might be a murderer, but unfortunately I can't do anything without speaking with our local counsel, first."

"I understand," Violet nodded. "Someone from the Metropolitan Police will be in touch."

Elise nodded and shook our hands as we left.

"Should we try to get footage from places around?" I asked, but Violet shook her head.

"I do not think it will do any good, at least not at the moment. The way the man stayed just outside of the view of the camera, even at the gym – he is always on the alert. He knows where the cameras are in the locales that he frequents; he would not have been caught on them."

"Right," I frowned. "That's a little bit annoying. I imagine it would be like trying to catch you."

Violet smiled at me. "I would not have let the police get this close."

"So you know who did it, then?"

"As I said, I have an idea. And as it forms, I get closer to the truth. But I will not say anything until I am certain. Now, we must wait for the warrant to arrive, and I will either confirm my suspicion, or discover that it is wrong."

"Well, at least we're somewhere."

"Yes, if we are lucky, we will know who it was who committed the crime by later tonight. I will call you when I have any more pertinent information."

"Okay," I said, before leaving and heading towards the underground station. It wasn't too far to get home, but a part of me really didn't want to go home right now. I was all too aware of the decision waiting for me, and I was going to keep procrastinating for as long as I could.

I pulled out my phone, and sent a text to Jake, not really expecting to hear back.

You around?

Doing the autopsy. You're welcome to come by if you want. Getting lunch soon.

I was already at Russell Square Station, since I knew the line would get me back to Glouchester Road and back home, but instead I got off at Green Park and transferred onto the Victoria line, which got me over to the mortuary where Jake worked.

When I walked into the basement, Jake was busy weighing organs.

"How's it going?" I asked, pulling up a stool to where Marnie Philips body lay, and having a look at what Jake was doing.

He shrugged. "So far, I don't have anything here that can help figure out who killed her. I know when she died, but I told Violet that at the crime scene. I can also tell you that she didn't have anything in her stomach at her time of death, and that she was strangled, but a six-year-old would've noticed the bruises on her neck. It's a little bit frustrating, I have to admit."

"Well, if it makes you feel any better, I'm pretty sure Violet has a suspect in mind."

"That does help, actually," Jake said. "I don't like knowing that someone is out there doing this to people. I hope whoever it is gets caught sooner rather than later."

"Same," I agreed. "Anyway, now we're waiting for a warrant so that we can get a list of the members of a certain gym in Bloomsbury where Marnie Philips met someone who is almost certainly the killer last night."

"Well, I'm happy for the company," Jake said. "I'm pretty sure I haven't slept in about two days, and I told my boss I'll be going for lunch soon because if I don't get out of here for an hour I'm going to go insane."

"Fair enough," I laughed. "I was going to text you yesterday, then figured you were too busy to come out."

"That's definitely accurate," Jake replied. "Let me just put Marnie here back in the freezer and I'll finish up after."

Ten minutes later we had made our way to The Marquis of Granby, a pub a couple of blocks away from the mortuary that was definitely a little bit on the fancier side while still maintaining a lot of that classic London charm. Jake and I managed to snag a small round table in the middle of the packed bar, and I looked around while Jake went to the bar to order food and drinks for us.

The place was dark, small, and packed to the brim. The low murmur of various conversations spread through the room like a hive of buzzing bees, while the sounds of tinkling glasses and cutlery on plates seemed to pierce through as well. It could've been annoying, but really, the cacophony of noise gave the place a warm feel, which was very welcome within the dark walls.

A few minutes later Jake came back with a couple of beers, and I took a long sip, not realizing until that moment just how much I could use that drink.

As I put my glass down and saw Jake still enjoying his, I figured he was in the exact same situation I was.

"So," Jake said with a grin. "Have you decided what you're going to do yet about your medical school applications?"

I let out a groan and leaned back in my chair. "You do realize I texted you because I didn't want to go home and have to face that same question, right?"

"A lesser man would be insulted by that, but yes, I'm completely aware. That's not going to make your problem go away, though. You said to me the other day that no matter what you want to make a decision for this semester."

"I did, and I kind of figured that as the deadline got closer I would figure out what to do. But I genuinely have no idea. What if I make the wrong decision?"

Jake shrugged. "Then you'll change. Lots of people make the wrong decision. When I was in school, I was sure I was going to become a lawyer. I actually did the first year of uni to become a lawyer before I realized I absolutely hated everything about it."

"Really?" I said, my eyebrows rising. "How come you never told me that before?"

Jake shrugged. "It wasn't really a big part of my life. I made a mistake, I changed paths, and during the year where I did a lot of random study I realized that I really, really enjoyed science. So I went into medicine, and I found my spot."

"What if I take the spot of someone who already

knows this is what they want to do, though?" I asked. "If I do become a doctor, don't I owe it to everybody who taught me anything to see it through?"

"No," Jake replied. "This is your life. And the fact that you're even thinking about it that way lets me know that you will be a great doctor. You're not one of those psychopaths that were only in it to feel like God; you genuinely feel for other people and think about how your actions affect them. That caring nature will make you a good doctor if you decide to go down that path, but it also means you need to take extra care to make sure you're doing what's best for you. Because in the end, this is your life. You don't want to get your deathbed and regret everything you've done because you thought that was what other people would want from you."

I looked into my half-drunk beer glass and realized Jake had a point. A really good point. In the end, this was my life. Shouldn't I do what was right for me, so long as it didn't affect other people in a negative way too badly?

My train of thought was interrupted by a waitress coming by with our food, and Jake and I spent the next ten minutes silently stuffing ourselves, me with fish and chips and him with a meat pie and fries.

"I don't think I'd ever been this hungry my life," Jake said when he finally finished the pie. "A part of me is really tempted to order another one, but I know I shouldn't."

I laughed. "If you're hungry, go for it. I won't judge."

"You're the best," he replied, planting a kiss on my cheek as he swept past me to make his way back to the bar. I was so thankful to have Jake my life. His advice was always on point, and I knew that if I ever needed to talk to him about anything, he was ready to listen and help in any way he could. It also helped that he wasn't that bad to look at.

When Jake came back, he grinned. "I couldn't bring myself to order a whole new pie, so I got us a bowl of sweet potato fries to share."

"I knew I loved you for a reason," I grinned, and my eyes widened immediately as I realized what I'd said. I had just told Jake I loved him. I had never done that before, and sure, it wasn't like I straight out said it. But it was close enough. I guess the thought of sweet potato fries had completely overridden my brain-to-mouth filter. I had to do something. "Sweet potato fries, I mean. I love sweet potato fries."

Super smooth. Way to brush past it completely naturally, Cassie. As I felt my face start to do a great impression of a tomato, I wanted to die. I wanted to sink under the table, curl up into a little ball, and never be seen again. I didn't even dare look at Jake; what on earth was wrong with me?

To my surprise, Jake just laughed. "You're ridiculous," he said. "I know you love sweet potato fries, and I love you too."

There was that warm, fuzzy feeling again.

CHAPTER 14

*T*wenty minutes later, we left the pub, with Jake having to get back to work. I still couldn't believe that had happened. Jake had told me he loved me! I was going to be honest: I had never had a boyfriend tell me he loved me before. This was huge.

There was a spring in my step as I kissed Jake goodbye and made my way back towards the underground station. I couldn't help it. Jake loved me! Plus, he had totally taken it in stride when I had embarrassed myself by accidentally saying it first.

Wasn't that true love? Finding someone who could take your embarrassing moments and make you feel like you were the most special person in the world?

I hopped back onto the train, but instead of going home, I decided that this was it. I was going to find *something* to get Violet for Christmas, no matter what. From Victoria Station it was just two quick stops to

Oxford Circus, which I knew was right in the center of trendy Soho. Surely I'd be able to find a cute little independent shop here that held something perfect for Violet.

I found myself, as all good nerds eventually do, inside the middle of Shapero Books, a bookstore and art gallery that felt like I had just stepped back into the library of a nineteenth century manor. I walked carefully up to a teal blue bookshelf filled with leather-bound volumes. An antique globe sat on a table in front of the window overlooking the street, and the wooden floorboards creaked beneath my feet. This was basically the perfect shop, and I suddenly had the perfect idea. I knew exactly what I was going to buy Violet for Christmas.

"Can I help you?" a woman about my age asked with a smile, and I turned to her.

"Yes, I know exactly what I'm looking for, and I hope you have it."

~

A couple of hours later, my gift bought and wrapped and carefully sitting inside one of my drawers at home where a mischievous Biscuit wouldn't be able to get to it, I got a text from Violet. *Warrant came through. I have the list of members. Come to my house.*

I left my spot on the couch, where I had been absolutely failing at watching Netflix, and instead stared at the TV while trying to figure out who on earth Violet could possibly suspect of having committed the crime. I hoped I was going to get my answer soon.

Giving Biscuit a quick pat as I left, I made my way to Violet's house, where I found her in the study, looking at a list of names on the computer.

"Is your suspect there?" I asked, and Violet nodded.

"He certainly is," she replied. "I am now one hundred percent certain that I know who our serial killer is. The problem is I do not yet know how to prove it."

"So who is it?" I asked, and Violet smiled at me.

"Do you not have the slightest idea yet?"

I shook my head. "Wouldn't have a clue."

"I can give you a clue. When was the first pacemaker created?"

"Nineteen-twenty-six," I replied instantly. "In Australia. It was first used to save a baby's life in 1928."

"And when was the last Sherlock Holmes book published."

I stared at Violet. "I have no idea. The thirties? I've read them, but it's not like I'm a huge fan or anything."

"Nineteen twenty seven. The first pacemaker in England was implanted in 1960. Therefore, there is no reason for one to have been left in the Sherlock Holmes Museum at the crime scene."

"You think it's a clue."

"I believe it was a taunt by our killer. He left it there

as a clue. It was a stupid mistake, but that is what gets them all in the end. The stupid mistakes. The killer who does not have an ego, the killer who is content to kill for killing's sake, he is the one who gets away with it. But this one, no. The pacemaker was a fatal flaw."

"The killer's a *doctor*?" I asked, incredulous. I knew there had been doctors who had been convicted of murder. But still, I had a hard time wrapping my head around the idea that someone who dedicated themselves to saving lives was also taking them.

"Yes," Violet replied matter-of-factly. "The killer is a doctor."

"Doctor King?" I asked, frowning slightly. He had seemed so normal when we met him, and yet if Violet said he was a murderer, he almost certainly was. She never said anything until she was sure.

"Indeed," Violet confirmed. "There are a few reasons why I believe him to be the killer. For one thing, he is on the list of members at the gym in Bloombsury. But I suspected him before then, as well."

"Why?"

"Well, for one thing, his entire demeanor. Psychopaths are often excellent at blending into society and acting the way people expect them to. When we saw him, doctor King was cordial, he was polite, and he was helpful. But it also took him a split second longer to speak than it would have for a regular person, and there were subtle clues in his demeanor that indicated to me that he was not exactly as he seemed. They would have been invisible to you, but for me, they were obvious. As soon as we met him, I knew the good doctor was not nearly as good as he pretended to be."

"I *knew* it," I said. "As soon as I saw him I stereotyped him as an arrogant butt, but then he was so nice I scolded myself for judging people before I got to know them."

Violet smiled. "Perhaps you should trust your instincts a little bit more." That definitely wasn't the first time I'd heard that saying over the last couple of days.

"So you knew as soon as we left the hospital that it was him?"

"*Non.* I only knew when we left the hospital that *docteur* King was not perhaps as good a man as he pretended to be. But, there are plenty of people who are similar, and who have not killed anyone."

"When did you figure it out, then?"

"I began to have suspicions after I saw the pacemaker in the museum. I know some of the people who work at that Museum, and I know that they would never be so reckless as to have something there that Doctor Watson would not have used. That was when I realized it had to be a hint from the killer, and it meant that our killer was most likely someone who worked in the medical field. Someone in the medical field would have known about the conference that Doctor Persson attended, and may have even been registered himself, which would have made it easier to steal the wallet.

However, when we went to visit Marnie Phillips' husband and he told us that she had not been to the hospital any time since returning from Australia, I began to think that perhaps my suspicions were wrong. However, the gym was the key. Doctor King was obviously in good shape, and evidently spent a great deal of time working out when he wasn't at the hospital. It made sense that the gym he attended would be near his work, and the fact that the gym at Bloomsbury was a twenty-four hour gym only worked more in favor of my theory. After all, Elise told us herself that a great deal of their clients are medical staff whose hours are not consistent."

I nodded. Everything Violet was saying made perfect sense, when she said it that way.

"The problem is, there is no way to prove anything I just said."

"Right," I nodded. "While it makes sense if you put everything together, individually, none of it is actual evidence."

"*Exactement.* If I go to DCI Kilmer now and tell him what we have discovered, he will not even be able to get an arrest warrant for Doctor King, let alone convict him of the two murders we know about."

"So what do you do now? We can't sit around and wait for him to kill someone else and hope he makes a mistake."

"No, we absolutely cannot. What we need to do is have him show himself and his true colors before he has the opportunity to kill again. We need to trap him so that he can be convicted of the crimes we know he has committed."

Well, that sounded super safe and easy. We were going to set a trap for a serial killer. What could possibly go wrong?

"he first thing we need to do is to find a target," Violet said. "I suspect that he will not attempt to kill me; not immediately, anyway. The body at the Sherlock Holmes Museum shows that he knows I am on this case, and he is taunting me. That was not a show put on for the police; that was a show put on for a private detective who occasionally helps the police. So, he is playing a game with me."

"Great, this is going to lead to me being poisoned or thrown out a window or something, isn't it?" I asked with a sigh.

Violet smiled at me. "Only if you are willing to do so. You really would be the perfect target: being my friend, going after you would be the perfect way for Doctor King to get under my skin."

"So what you're saying is if I don't do this, other people are going to die?"

"Not necessarily," Violet said. "I do not want you to do this if you are not comfortable with it. But I will do everything in my power to make sure you stay safe. There are other ways; I believe this to be the easiest, however."

I sighed. To be totally honest, I really did not want to do this. I had never been an especially adventurous type, and throwing myself into the lion's den of a serial killer that we knew was taunting Violet didn't sound particularly appealing to me.

On the other hand, if I died, at least I would never have to make a decision about medical school.

Shoving that morbid thought aside, I considered what I was going to do in reality. On the one hand, I absolutely did not want to do this. There was a very real risk that I was going to become the target of the serial killer, but at the same time, what if I didn't do this and someone else died? I would never be able to live with myself knowing that I could've done something about it, but that my own cowardice had prevented me from stopping a killer before it was too late.

Two people were already dead. I had to do whatever I could to stop that number from becoming three. Even if it meant sacrificing my own safety for a little while.

Besides, I knew Violet. I knew if anybody was going to be able to stop Doctor King, it was her. And if anybody was going to be able to stop him from killing me, again, it was her.

"I'll do it," I said before I had a chance to talk myself out of it.

Violet nodded, as if she knew that was what I was going to do the entire time. "Good. This will make it easier to stop him, and it will hopefully not take too long."

"Can we do this in a way that doesn't involve too much pain on my part?" I asked. "With my knee, I have to say I've experienced enough pain for one lifetime."

"It would be easier if you were willing to break a bone."

"No! No, absolutely not."

Violet shrugged. "It only hurts for a little bit."

"It does not! Have you forgotten that I am practically a doctor? I know how the human body works, and I've seen a lot of broken bones. I've even broken them myself. I know how much they hurt. Come up with something else."

"Fine," Violet said. "We will do it with less pain. Are you able to fake dizziness and weakness properly?"

"I think so," I replied.

"Good," Violet said, standing up. "Then, we go back to the crime scene at Baker Street, since it makes sense that we would be there, and that is where you will have your injury."

"Are you at least going to tell me what that injury is

going to be?" I asked. "Dizziness and weakness makes me think blood loss."

"Very good, doctor," Violet replied with a smile, and I had to admit, I was a little bit worried. At least she said faking. That was something, right?

~

Half an hour later we were back at the crime scene, having made our way past the police officer guarding the door at the bottom and back into the room where Marnie Phillips's body had been found. The scene looked almost identical to the way it had when I was last in this room, except that the body had been moved, there was mud on the floor that had been tracked in by the various law enforcement officials that had come by, and everything was covered in a thin layer of black fingerprint dust.

My eyes were immediately drawn to the pacemaker, which was still sitting where it had been the last time I had seen it. Violet's eyes followed mine, and she scoffed.

"Of course they would not realize that was a crucial piece of evidence and not simply one of the artifacts in this museum," she muttered. "I will have to text DCI Kilmer and have one of his men come over and take it into evidence; it may come in useful later on."

"At least they took fingerprints from it," I said,

motioning to the black dust on top of the piece of metal.

"There will not have been anything on that pace-maker," Violet said. "Doctor King was much too careful for that."

"Okay, so what are we going to do here?"

"I want to cut your scalp open slightly," Violet said, and I balked. That was definitely not a sentence you ever wanted to hear your best friend say to you.

"Seriously?"

"The more blood, the better."

"Then cut my inner arm or something,"

"The head bleeds better than anywhere else in the body due to the high concentration of blood vessels, and you know it."

I sighed. I did know it, and I knew Violet was right. Head injuries were often not at all serious, but they bled like crazy, which was exactly what we wanted.

"Fine," I finally conceded. "Please make it quick, though."

Violet nodded and made her way into Sherlock Holmes's kitchen, coming back with a long, serrated knife. "This should do fine," she said, pulling a large container of disinfectant from her purse. I watched as she made her way over to the sink, putting in the plug, and poured in the disinfectant and dropped the knife in. At least I wasn't going to die of an infection after we did this.

"I guess we have twenty minutes to kill?" I asked, and Violet nodded.

"Yes, by then the blade will be perfectly safe to use."

"What's the rest of the plan?" I asked. "We go to the hospital, they close up my wound, and then what? We don't even know that Doctor King is working today."

"*You* do not know that Doctor King is working today. I called the hospital earlier and asked, making sure that he was in accident and emergency all day. I would not do something so invasive to you if I was not sure. As for the rest of the plan, I think it is better if you do not know. Besides, planning things like this too carefully often leads to making mistakes. If I have the right plan that is easily modifiable to any situation, that is much better than something that has been planned too carefully. It is always good to be flexible when hunting a killer."

"That's code for you have absolutely no idea, isn't it?" I said with a small smile.

"No, it is not. There is a difference between having a plan that is open and flexible, and having no plan at all. I would not send you as a potential victim if I had no plan at all."

"Okay," I agreed. "Are you coming to the hospital with me when I cut myself?"

"Of course," Violet replied. "However, when you are discharged, I will be leaving separately from you. I would like you to mention to Doctor King that you will be going back to the Sherlock Holmes Museum to look at the crime scene as you think you may have remembered something and you want to be certain. When you are discharged, stop and get some food - I do not think finding something will be difficult for you - and then make your way to the museum."

I nodded. "Sounds good. Got it."

"Are you ready," Violet said, taking the knife out from the disinfectant. "I cannot promise that this will not hurt, but I will do my best to find an area that will bleed without hurting too much."

"Well, what are friends for?" I replied with a grin. I couldn't help but think about the absolute ridiculousness of the situation, in which my best friend was about to slice open my head so that I could get admitted to the hospital straight away.

"Sit down over there, and hold still," Violet ordered, directing me towards one of the chairs. I sat on the edge of it, not wanting my blood to get on any of the items in this room. After all, this was still a working museum. Closing my eyes, I focused on my breathing and did my best not to move at all while Violet carefully moved my hair aside, trying to find the spot where she wanted to make the cut.

"Here I go," she said, and I let out a breath slowly as the cold metal of the knife sliced my scalp.

I instinctively let out a whine, but to be honest, it didn't hurt nearly as much as I thought it would have. Still, a moment later I could feel a warm liquid running down through my hair, and I knew it was my own blood.

"Here," Violet said to me, handing me a small hand-kerchief. "Use this to staunch the bleeding, I have a car waiting downstairs to take us straight to the hospital."

I jumped to my feet and instantly and felt a tiny bit dizzy; Violet had obviously managed to make a good cut if I was losing blood this quickly. I was starting to wonder if this had really been a good idea after all.

CHAPTER 16

Sure enough, as soon as we got downstairs there was a man across the street with his hazard lights on, driving a Toyota Avensis – basically a Camry with a different name, because that was what marketing people did - that was maybe five years old. Violet led me straight to the car, and I got in, holding the handkerchief tightly to my head to try and avoid dripping on the man's upholstery. I could already feel wetness on the other side of the handkerchief; it was obviously completely soaked with blood.

"Right, to the hospital then?" the man asked, and Violet nodded.

"*Oui,* thank you, Ronald."

"Always happy to do you a favor, Violet," Ronald replied. "Goodness knows you've done enough for me."

Ronald sped off, driving especially aggressively, even by central London standards. As a result, we got to the hospital only a few minutes later, and Ronald dropped us off at the entrance to accident and emergency.

"See you later," he said, leaving as soon as Violet and I stepped out of the car. He had never once asked who I was, or why I was bleeding profusely from my head.

Violet and I made our way inside, and found that the nurse at reception was the same one we had spoken to the other day, who had told us about Doctor King in the first place. Her eyes sparked with recognition as soon as she saw us, but then she quickly went into nursing mode.

"Come with me, we need to get the bleeding stopped on this wound as quickly as possible."

I followed after her, and Violet tapped me lightly on the arm. "If you are going to collapse, now would be a good time."

I nodded. A simple head wound was basically nothing, I knew that all too well. They bled like crazy, but they often weren't serious, and I knew that Violet hadn't sliced deeply at all. Any nurse would be able to tell that I just needed a few stitches and for the bleeding to stop, and that I would be fine. On the other hand, if I were to fall and find myself unconscious for a minute, that might indicate a concussion, or something worse. In that case, I was definitely going to see a doctor.

I took a deep breath and closed my eyes, then forced my shoe to hit the tile just a little bit wrong, sending me flying forward. I actually did a much better job of crashing than I had planned or expected to; I was going to simply slide on the floor, and catch myself, but instead my foot that caught hit my other foot, which knocked me off balance and sent me actually careening towards the floor for real.

Like an idiot, I reached out instinctively with my arm to stop the fall, and as soon as it hit the ground, a searing pain shot through my wrist and up to my shoulder.

Great. This was exactly what I had told Violet I didn't want to do on purpose, and now I had just done it by accident.

"Argh," I cried out, grabbing at my injured arm, and the nurse stopped and looked, horrified. This was definitely feeling like a worse and worse idea by the second.

"I need a wheelchair here, now!" the nurse called out, and a minute later someone else in scrubs came by with a wheelchair, with Violet and the two nurses helping me into it. At this point, I was in enough pain that I wasn't paying attention to much, but I did realize I'd lost my handkerchief at some point, because blood began pooling down my face and I was too busy clutching at my injured wrist to wipe it away.

What on earth had I been thinking in agreeing to this plan? We hadn't even come across the serial killer yet and I already felt like I was dying.

I was quickly wheeled over to a bed, where the

nurse who brought in the wheelchair immediately set about to stop the bleeding, while the other went left, presumably to go back to reception. The nurse was male, about thirty-five, with friendly eyes.

"Lie down on the bed, please," he told me as he pulled on latex gloves and pressed a large strip of gauze against the cut. "What caused this cut?"

"A knife," Violet said. "I was holding it near her while she was crouched down, and she stood up and inadvertently sliced her head on it."

"Right," the nurse said. "Was the knife dirty at all?"

"No, I had just cleaned it," Violet replied. I supposed it would have sounded pretty sketchy to admit to sterilizing a knife before slicing someone's head open with it.

"Ok," the nurse replied.

"I can hold the gauze if you want," I offered. I was well aware that it was going to have to stay in place for at least fifteen minutes.

"Sorry, this one's my job," the nurse said with a smile. "I'm Khalim, by the way."

"Cassie," I said with a smile. "Hey, Violet, can you go give my information at reception and get me checked in?"

"Yes, that is a good idea," Violet replied, and I handed her my purse, which I was sad to see had gotten a few drops of blood on it. Hopefully washing them out wouldn't be too hard.

"It's going to need stitches, isn't it?" I asked.

"It's possible, but I'm not sure yet," Khalim replied. "You're actually quite lucky. This cut is clean, and while it is long, it is quite narrow."

"Small mercies, I guess," I replied with a small smile. At least Violet knew exactly how to cut me to minimize the odds of having stitches carved into my scalp later.

The next few minutes passed in a bit of a daze. Twenty minutes later, the bleeding in my scalp had stopped, and Violet had come back as well.

"The doctor will be here shortly," Khalim told me as he removed the gauze from my head and confirmed that the bleeding had mostly stopped. "He wants to have a look at you, and make sure you're not concussed, since the fall is a little bit worrying. Then, we'll send you in for X-rays."

"Thank you," I said to Khalim, and he nodded and left to take care of other patients.

"This had better be worth it," I hissed to Violet as he left.

"You did not have to be so convincing with your wrist."

"I'm not faking it. I legitimately think I broke something."

Violet raised her eyebrows. "I did think the fall looked especially good for a fake. How on earth did you manage to trip over your own two feet?"

"I don't know," I said glumly. "It just happened."

"Well, whatever the reason, it is good that it

happened, as it means you are definitely going to be seen by *docteur* King now."

"Great," I muttered. I knew that was the goal, but right now, I was just in too much pain to really care about proving he was a serial killer.

"Well, no matter. The end goal has been achieved: you are in the hospital, and you will be seen by the doctor."

I nodded, my mouth suddenly going dry. It was one thing to have come up with this plan in theory, it was entirely another to know that I was about to face a man who had killed two people that we knew of, but probably a lot more.

Still, when, about five minutes later, the privacy curtain was pulled back and Doctor King smiled at me, I immediately resisted the urge to throw up all over him and instead flashed him a smile.

"Well, well, well. What have we here? I wasn't expecting to see you back so soon, and certainly not as a patient rather than as an investigator," the doctor said when he entered the room. He smiled cordially at Violet and nodded, and she replied with a sweet smile of her own that reached her eyes. She was nothing if not an excellent actress.

I took my cue from her and tried to plaster an embarrassed smile on my face.

"Yes, well, unfortunately things didn't go exactly as planned."

"I trust you're getting closer to finding the killer?"

"Oh, we are quite close," Violet said. "I suspect the police will be making an arrest soon. The killer should be very careful."

I studied Doctor King's face closely as Violet said those words, and maybe I imagined it, but I could have sworn I saw his left eyebrow twitch just a tiny little bit.

"Is that so? Well, that's excellent news," he replied without skipping a beat. "Now, let me have a look at that cut."

My body tensed up involuntarily as Doctor King made his way towards me and touched my scalp, but if he noticed, he made no mention of it. "Hmm, yes, that isn't too bad a cut after all. They do bleed like crazy, though, those ones. Now, the nurse mentioned that you collapsed coming in. Does your head hurt at all?"

I shook my head as I answered the rest of Doctor King's questions as he ascertained whether or not I had a concussion. "Well, I think you're clear when it comes to concussion," he finally said. "Luckily for you, there's only the cut. I'd like to give you a few stitches, because if that wound reopens on its own it's going to be quite painful, but I'll make them dissolvable stitches so that you won't need to return and have them taken out."

"Thank you, Doctor," I said, trying not to freak out at the fact that a serial killer was about to go at my head with the needle.

"Before we do that, though, I want to get that wrist x-rayed. Stay here, and one of the technicians will come to get you shortly."

Doctor King left, and Violet put a finger to her lips as soon as he did, waited about thirty seconds, then checked to make sure that he had actually left the area.

"There. Now we know that he is not listening in to what we are saying," Violet said.

"He's cool as a cucumber, that's for sure," I said with a low whistle. "I think I saw his eyebrow twitch when you said that we were close to an arrest, but that was it."

"So you noticed that as well," Violet said with a nod. "Good. Good observational skills. I believe we have definitely gotten under his skin, but at the same time, I suspect he has no idea that we mean him to be the main suspect."

"Isn't that the whole point of us coming here? So that he knows that we believe he's the killer?"

Violet shook her head. "No. The psychology of the arrogant serial killer who wants attention is that they need to get the attention. They crave recognition for what they have done, but they still want to get away with it. If we thought Doctor King was a serial killer, why would we come back here? Why would we tell him we thought we were close to an arrest? No, everything I said was to tell him that I have somebody else in mind as the killer. That, more than anything, is going to drive him to fixate on us - to fixate on you."

"Great," I muttered.

"He will want to get closer to me, to punish me for

giving the credit for this crime to somebody else. This is the best way to get him to focus on us."

Before I had a chance to respond, a tall, rather chubby woman with a friendly face and a warm smile pulled aside the privacy curtain.

"Cassie?" she asked. "I'm here to take you to get x-rays. You're alright to walk, right?"

"I am," I said with a smile as I got up off the bed, carefully holding my wrist.

"Perfect. Follow me and we'll get that wrist looked at straight away."

hirty minutes later, Violet and I were waiting in the room once more. I'd had the X-rays taken; the nurse was quite nice and asked a lot about San Francisco, telling me she wished she could go there for Christmas as the weather seemed "quite a bit nicer than this gloomy lot."

I had to admit, I kind of agreed. I had lived in the Bay Area my entire life, and for me, December meant cooler weather, sure, and the occasional bout of rain, but it was still primarily sunshine central.

Here in London, however, while it had started to be sunny once more, in November and the first few days of December there had come a time when it felt like I was never going to see the sun again. I had come to love the overcast days, because at least it wasn't raining, and it seemed like it took every effort in the world to get out of bed on some of those days. It felt a lot more like I had when I first moved to London, until luckily, eventually Violet noticed that I wasn't going out much and suggested I take some vitamin D tablets.

"It is not easy, living in this climate in the winter, for someone like you who comes from the warm weather," Violet explained.

"How on earth do you do it?" I asked.

"I come to appreciate the various aspects of each season individually. It is not possible to properly appreciate the warmth of the first true summer's day if one has not suffered through the three previous months of a cold winter."

"Speak for yourself, I appreciate warm days all the time," I muttered.

"But you have not yet spent a winter here. Wait until May, when we have the first truly warm spring day. You will bask in the sun in a way that you could not imagine having enjoyed it every day of your life up until now."

"Ok, we'll see," I said skeptically. Now, however, as the weather got even colder as the clouds opened up and revealed the sun once more, I couldn't help but wonder if Violet was right. I would give anything for a good ninety-degree day on the beach right now. Would I really appreciate the sun more now that I had gone so long without truly experiencing its warmth?

As soon as I left the X-ray area and was brought back to my hospital bed, however, my mind turned back to the crime. Doctor King would be back again soon. Was my wrist really broken? It certainly felt like it was. How was that going to affect how I was going to solve the case? Being one arm down certainly couldn't be an advantage when trying to catch a killer.

Still, hopefully it wouldn't come to that. Violet was really more of a chess player than a boxer; she would always try to trap someone using her intelligence rather than her brute force.

"Right," Doctor Knight said when he came back in. "You have a distal radius fracture after all, but you're lucky. It's a simple break, which doesn't need any resetting. There's enough swelling that I'd like to start by putting the wrist in a splint, and then have you come back in a couple of days for a cast."

I nodded; all of what Doctor King said made perfect sense, and didn't sound like it was coming from a serial killer at all. I wanted to kick myself inwardly for having fallen like that. This was going to take weeks to heal, I knew that all too well. How could I have been so stupid?

"Make sure to keep your wrist elevated when possible, ice it frequently, and take some over-the-counter painkillers like ibuprofen when needed for pain."

I nodded, barely listening. I knew all of this, of course. I had never introduced myself to Doctor King as an almost-doctor, though, so there was no way for him to know that I knew exactly how to take care of what was one of the most common bone breaks in the human body.

A few minutes later, he left, and Khalim came back to splint my arm.

By the time Violet and I left the hospital, it was almost one in the afternoon.

"Well, this is a lot more annoying than I had expected," I said to Violet, waving my newly-splinted arm at her. "Who knew that I was going to *actually* need an emergency room visit today?"

"All the same, it is convenient. A broken wrist means there is no way Doctor King could suspect anything from our visit, and it makes you a better target for him, as you are now weaker."

"Yeah, that's great," I replied sarcastically. "What do I do now?"

Violet checked her watch. "While you were in with the technician getting the X-ray done, I went back to the front reception area and was able to glean that the good doctor's shift ends in twenty minutes. I will leave, but I would like you to stay out here for that long, at least. The easier we make it for him to track you, the better."

"The more this goes on, the more I wish you were the bait."

"I do not make good bait," Violet replied. "It must be someone close to me. Do not worry. No matter what happens, I will not be far."

I sighed as Violet got into a cab and drove off. I couldn't help but think as the car sped away that she was definitely further away than I was happy with.

Still, I had to trust her. Innocent lives were at stake. Wasn't this what a doctor did? They did whatever they could to save their patients. Right now, everyone in the city of London was my patient. The difference was, most doctors didn't put their lives at stake to save people.

I had to convince myself that this was the right thing to do, because to be totally honest, a part of me felt like running away screaming as far away from Violet as I could possibly get.

Instead, I sat on a concrete pillar and checked the time. I texted Brianne, who was working, but her shift ended in an hour. I figured if anyone deserved Chipotle right now, it was me.

"What happened to you?" Brianne asked in horror when I walked into Chipotle forty minutes later. I had waited longer than the twenty minutes, just to be on the safe side, then walked over to Brianne's job, resisting the urge to look over my shoulder every two seconds.

"I tripped and fell," I said miserably. "And also, Violet sliced my head open with a knife this morning to help find a serial killer, so this has definitely not been a ten out of ten day."

"Well, if I've ever heard a reason to give someone free guac, this is it," Brianne said with a sympathetic shake of her head.

I laughed. "That makes it all worth it."

"I knew the promise of guacamole would make you

feel better," Brianne grinned as she assembled my burrito bowl. She knew my order off by heart, there was no need for me to tell her what I wanted.

"I'll wait for you to get off shift," I said. "You have no idea the day I've had."

"I definitely need to hear all about it," Brianne said.

I ate my burrito bowl, wondering if between the splint and the dried blood on my hair I didn't look like way too much of a crazy person to be out in public, and Brianne eventually sat down in front of me, her work clothes gone.

"Be honest, on a scale from one to ten, how much of a crazy person do I look like right now?"

"Probably a three," Brianne replied after studying me for a moment. "There's a bit of blood in your hair, and you wouldn't suffer from running a brush through it, but apart from that you look fine."

"Thank goodness for small mercies," I muttered.

"For sure, but now you have to tell me everything," Brianne drawled, leaning forward on the table. I looked around to make sure none of the nearby spots were occupied. Confident that we weren't about to be over-heard, I told Brianne everything that had happened that day, including the fact that we had figured out who the killer was. I wasn't afraid of her leaking the name or anything like that. Brianne was as trustworthy as they came.

Her eyes got so wide by the time I got to the end of

the story I thought there was a very real risk they were going to pop out of her head.

"That's insane," she finally said when I finished, her voice barely more than a whisper. "You are insane. What is wrong with you?"

"What?"

"You've literally just put yourself in the path of a serial killer in the hopes that he'll target you to be his next victim. Do you not understand how completely insane that is?"

"Of course I do. But, if I don't do it, someone else is going to be killed before we can prove that Doctor King is the killer."

"So? This way has a really high chance of you dying. I mean, I'm all for adventures and trying to solve crimes and all that sort of thing, but you have to think about yourself. You're putting yourself in serious danger here, Cassie, and I'd hate to think that anything bad could ever happen to you."

I had to admit, I was pretty touched by Brianne's words. Still, I knew that despite the fact that what she said did make some sense, I had to keep going anyway. I had to do this, because it was the only way to stop a killer before he struck again.

"That's the problem though," I said. "If there's a chance that I can do something, even if it means putting myself in danger, I have to do it. I would never be able to live with myself if I had said no and someone else was killed. Besides, Violet knows where I am, and she knows to keep track of me. I've got to be the safest piece of bait in all of London."

Brianne shook her head. "You're insane, you know that? If it wasn't for the fact that I have to do a bunch of stuff in the hospital tonight, I would 100% not be leaving your side."

"You just finished telling me about how dangerous what I'm doing is and how I absolutely shouldn't do it," I said, crossing my arms in front of me.

"Yeah, because it's you. I don't think you should do it, but I have no problem putting myself in harm's way either."

"You are absolutely ridiculous," I said with a smile as I took a big swig from my container of Coke. "Only you would tell me not to do something and then bemoan the fact that you can't do it yourself."

"I'm not good bait, anyway," Brianne said with a sigh. "For as much as I hate what you're doing right now, Violet is definitely right. It has to be you who's the bait so that the killer can get close to her."

"Right, I vote we stop talking about this completely, because I really don't like being spoken about like a worm on a hook for a fish."

"And when I'm at your funeral I don't want this to be the last conversation we had," Brianne replied.

"That's not helping."

"It's not supposed to help, I still think this is a terrible idea and I think you should back out now."

"Well, I'm not going to. I need to do this, because we

don't have any other choice. This guy's going to kill someone again, and probably soon. If he doesn't come after me, he's going to come after someone else, and I just can't have that."

"Well, if you're not dead, come stop by my hospital in a few days and I'll put your cast on you," Brianne said. "I'm working in radiology for the next few weeks, so I'll give you the nice bright pink one that we keep for little girls. It's actually super cute and looks way better than the plain white most adults get."

"Deal," I grinned. I wasn't an especially girly girl, but if I was going to have to keep a cast on for a few weeks, I was totally on board with getting something that stood out a little bit instead of being just plain white.

"Okay," Brianne said. "I've got to get going, but if you get into any trouble at all, I want you to call me. I will 100% answer my phone no matter what, even if I'm in the middle of giving someone CPR to save their life."

I burst out laughing at the mental image. "I think they might not give you your medical license if you let somebody die so you could answer a phone call."

"It would be worth it, though, if it meant saving your life," Brianne replied. "I mean it. Call me anytime."

"Thanks," I said to her with a smile. "You're a great friend, you know that?"

"I do," Brianne replied, not a hint of modesty in her body. "But I don't have a lot of friends, which is why I want to keep the ones I have. Try not to die tonight."

"I'll do my best," I replied earnestly.

Brianne got up and left the shop, making her way up the street where I knew she was going to catch the tube to get to the hospital. I leaned back in my seat and sighed. I didn't want to admit it, but Brianne's words had gotten to me. I also realized that I hadn't told Jake yet what Violet and I were doing. Didn't I owe it to him to let him know? After all, he loved me. He really loved me. I owed him this much, at least.

Pulling out my phone, I dialed his number but it went through to voicemail. This wasn't the sort of thing you could tell someone in a message.

I hung up, frowning at the phone. A part of me figured maybe I should go see him in person, but then that was pretty far from this area, which seemed to be where Doctor King did his hunting for victims. Maybe I could just call him again in a few minutes, instead.

Eventually, I sighed and decided it was time to get going. I picked up my tray and went to bus it, but as I passed the chair where Brianne had been sitting, I noticed her keys sitting on the chair. They must have fallen out of her pocket without her noticing.

I grabbed her keys, pulled out my phone, and sent her a text.

Hey dummy, you left your keys here at Chipotle. Want me to come by the hospital and drop them off?

Sure, going to the hospital where Brianne worked was definitely going to be a little bit further out of the way than I wanted to go, but it was only going to be for a few minutes, and then I could come back here under the guise of revisiting the crime scene at the Sherlock Holmes Museum. Brianne needed her keys, after all.

But when a few minutes had passed, and Brianne hadn't answered my text, I began to wonder what was going on.

CHAPTER 18

*W*hat happened to answering my phone calls
immediately?

I added a tongue poking out emoji and sent the text.
I wasn't exactly worried; Brianne was probably just
walking along and hadn't heard her phone.

When a couple of minutes later, however, she still
hadn't answered that text either, I frowned. I should
call her, just in case I could catch her before she got on
the train. It would save me a trip to the hospital,
after all.

Dialing her number, she answered a minute later.

"Oh, hey Cassie," she said.

"Well, I guess you did promise only answer the
phone, and not my texts," I joked. "You left your keys at
the restaurant, are you on the train yet?"

"Uh, yeah," Brianne said. "That was silly of me. I'm

on the train now, but don't worry about the keys. I can come by your place later and pick them up."

"Oh don't worry about it," I said. "I'll come by the hospital and drop them off."

"Okay, cool, thanks. If you just leave them with one of the nurses at reception that would be great; I'm going to be stuck in the oncology ward all night. It's too bad, I wanted to show you the cool blue cast I'm going to put on your arm when that swelling goes down."

Alarm bells went off in my head. Brianne had just finished telling me that she was going to be working in radiology, not oncology, and she wanted to give me a pink cast, not a blue one. Straight away, my mind focused on what I should do next. I could hear sounds in the background, and sirens somewhere. Brianne was talking to me on speakerphone, which meant that if someone had her, they were listening in to this conversation too.

That was when I realized who it was.

Doctor King. It had to be. He wasn't going to use me as his next victim, he was going after Brianne.

My heart sunk in my chest as the realization dawned upon me. If she was on speakerphone, there was nothing I could say that he wouldn't overhear. How on earth was I going to get a message to her without him realizing I'd figured it out?

I probably wasn't going to be able to. She was just going to have to trust that I understood her message and that I was going to come after her. Because if one thing was for certain, it was that I wasn't going to let one of my best friends become this serial killer's next victim.

"Sounds good," I said to her. "I'll drop them off as soon as I can. After all, what are friends for? I got you."

"You're the best," Brianne said.

"Talk to you soon, promise," I said.

"Bye."

As the line went dead when Brianne hung up, I couldn't help but feel an intense amount of guilt and fear. How on earth were we going to find Brianne? And how long do we have before Doctor King killed her?

Straight away, I went into Doctor mode. This was an emergency. Sure, it was an emergency that included one of my best friends, but it was an emergency all the same. I had to put aside all of my emotions and focus on doing what I had to to get her back as quickly as possible.

I dialed Violet's number straight away.

"Yes?"

"He has Brianne," I said.

"You are certain?"

"Absolutely. I think she's in a car with him. How are we going to find her?"

"Brianne has an iPhone," Violet said. "You would not by chance know her password, would you?"

"No," I replied breathlessly. "Why?"

"The fastest way to track her will be by using 'find

your iPhone,' especially if we know she still has it on her. Let me see if I can get into her account quickly. I will call you back shortly. Cassie, she will be alright. We will find her."

Violet hung up the phone and I found myself pacing in front of the Chipotle on Baker Street, feeling completely useless.

Brianne was out there, having been taken by a serial killer, and it was all my fault. There was no doubt about that. Doctor King had almost certainly followed me from the hospital, and then seen me speaking with Brianne, and decided that it was probably safer to take her than to take me.

And after warning me that what I was doing was stupid and far too dangerous, too.

Wracked with guilt, I tried to figure out what could have happened. Brianne had been gone for fewer than five minutes when I called her, so there was a very limited period of time in which something bad could've happened.

In fact, she wouldn't even have had time to walk up to Baker Street station. And the sounds on the phone were not those of someone who was in the underground. Besides, I didn't think Doctor King would have kidnapped her there. The London Underground was covered in CCTV cameras, and up until now, we had had zero luck in finding him on tape. He obviously knew to stay away from the cameras, which meant that he would absolutely stay away from public transport.

That meant he had to have a car. That would make sense; it had seemed pretty quiet in the background when I was on the phone with Brianne, not at all like I would expect in the London Underground. But it did fit with a car.

I made my way up the street, looking around, trying to find somebody who might've noticed something. As I looked towards a bakery with a woman in the window kneading away at some dough, I smiled. Jackpot. Hopefully, she had seen something.

I made my way into the bakery, where a different woman smiled at me.

"Hi there, what can I get for you today?"

"Sorry," I said. "I'm wondering if either one of you happened to see a woman getting into a car near here maybe ten minutes ago?"

"A redhead?" The woman by the window asked and I nodded enthusiastically.

"Yes, her. What can you tell me? Please, it's very important."

"Well, a car pulled up next to her a few minutes ago. She didn't look like she knew the driver, but he spoke to her for a minute, and then she got into the passenger seat."

"What kind of car was it?" I asked.

"It was a late-model BMW five series, silver," the woman replied. "That's basically my dream car, which is why I noticed exactly what type it was."

"Do you have any idea which way it went? And you

didn't catch the license plate number by any chance, did you?"

"Sorry," the woman said, shaking her head. "I wouldn't have a clue. I didn't think there was anything untoward about it, so the car just drove off. It did turn right on Marylebone, though," she added.

"Thank you, thank you so much," I said, rushing out of the shop as my phone began to ring. It was Violet.

"Do you have anything?"

"I have managed to access Brianne's phone account. I have her phone. It was thrown out of the car she was in next to Great Portland Street station, with Doctor King most likely hoping that someone would pick it up and continue to use it."

"I'll be there in a couple of minutes," I said, rushing out to the intersection and flagging down a cab.

"There's an extra twenty in it for you if you get me to Great Portland Street station in two minutes," I said to the cabbie. If it wasn't for the fact that one of my best friends was in trouble, I would've felt totally cool using one of those classic moving lines. Rush hour was starting now, and this section of London was notorious for having bad traffic at the best of times, but my cabbie was definitely motivated to get me to Violet as quickly as possible. At one point he even went into the oncoming traffic lane in order to pass an exceptionally slow-moving delivery van.

Every second seemed to be an eternity, but it couldn't have taken more than two minutes for us to finally get in front of the station, where I saw Violet looking out for me.

"Thank you," I practically shouted at the cab driver as I tossed a twenty and a five onto the seat next to him and jumped out.

"Do you have anything else?" I asked Violet. "He's driving a silver BMW five series."

"Unfortunately, so are half the drivers in this city," Violet replied. "We could get the CCTV footage from around here and hope to track his car, but that will take far too much time. No, we need to get to Brianne fast. She does not have much time before he will kill her.

CHAPTER 19

"So what do we do? We can't track her with her phone. He has to be around here, doesn't he? Everything he has done has been in this neighborhood. This is where he's most comfortable."

"Yes, I agree," Violet said. "We need a computer, and we need it now. I have called DCI Williams, and he will be here in just a couple of minutes."

Luckily for both of us, Paddington Green police station was not far from where we were at the moment, and three excruciating minutes later DCI Williams pulled up in front of us, lights and sirens blaring.

"Get out," Violet ordered as soon as he pulled up to the curb, and the rather startled -looking police detectives did as she ordered, with Violet slipping into the driver's seat and opening up the police computer straight away.

"What's going on?" DCI Williams asked me while Violet typed away.

"One of my best friends has been kidnapped by the man who killed the people at King's Cross and at the Sherlock Holmes Museum."

DCI Williams' mouth dropped open. "You're joking."

"I wish I was," I said glumly. "I was supposed to be the bait, but he took her instead."

"I don't even want to know what that bait sentence means," DCI Williams said. "What is Violet looking for? Can I help?"

"I have no idea," I said, and a second later noticed Violet motioning for me to come over.

"Get in," she told me and I slipped into the passenger seat. I hadn't even managed to completely close the door before Violet was speeding off through traffic, lights and sirens blaring.

Yeah, she had definitely just stolen a police car. As I looked in the side mirror and saw DCI Williams running after us, shouting something that we had no chance of being able to hear, I wondered just how much trouble Violet was going to get into for this particular stunt.

I seriously hoped it was going to be worth it.

"Where are we going?" I asked.

"Doctor King's apartment is not too far from here. However, I do not think that he has gone there to kill Brianne. Do you remember what he said to us when we spoke to him the first time about Joseph Fenman?"

"Sure, I remember most of that conversation."

"At one point, he mentioned that the view over-looking the park was very beautiful."

"So?"

"So, Regent's Park is not the London Eye, and it is not the Champs de Mars in Paris, either. It is rather residential for being in central London, and there are not many opportunities to overlook the park."

"You're thinking that he has an apartment near there," I said, my mind working at warp speed.

"I do think that, yes," Violet said. "In fact, thanks to the database available in the police car, I am certain of it."

"Where is it?"

"On Prince Albert Road, in Consort Lodge," Violet explained. "Did you notice his tattoo at the hospital? It featured a galah, a grey and pink parrot native to Australia."

"I did, I thought it looked weird at the time," I nodded.

"They are not a common bird. I did a broad search of property records for the streets around Regent Park, and one of the apartments is owned by a company called Eolophus Inc. Seeing as the Latin name for the Galah is *eolophus roseicapilla*, that is far too much of a coincidence for my liking. I am willing to bet that the company is owned entirely by Doctor King, and that it is where he takes his victims to kill them. It fits the location, what he mentioned about overlooking the park, and I do know the building. It has an underground car park, making it easy for a killer to transport a body elsewhere."

I felt sick at the thought that this was where Brianne was being held before Doctor King killed her, but at the same time, I was hopeful that we were going to find her there, safe and sound.

Violet cut the lights and siren as we got closer to the building. "I will park around the corner; I do not want him noticing either the police car, or our arrival. The element of surprise is the best thing we have in this situation, and we must not waste it."

Suddenly, Violet's phone began to ring, and as it was sitting next to her on the Centre console, I glanced at the screen.

"DCI Williams wants to know what you're doing with his police car," I said to her.

"He will simply have to wait. This is an emergency. I am sure he will understand as soon as I explain everything."

"You had better hope so, since I don't think stealing a police car is going to go down very well, even if it is to catch a serial killer before he kills again."

Violet waved away my worries as she parked the car in a commercial zone on Albert Terrace and the two of us got out. I could feel my heart pounding in my chest as we continued along, a park on either side of us.

"Is this all part of The Regent's Park?" I asked, motioning around, but Violet shook her head.

"No. The park to our left is Primrose Hill. As soon as we pass it, we will be at the building we are looking for."

We power-walked, with me barely noticing the pain in my knee that always appeared when I exerted myself a little bit too much. What was a little bit of pain compared to Brianne's life?

As soon as we reached the corner that marked the end of Primrose Hill Park, Violet held out a hand to stop me from going further.

"We cannot simply storm in and expect to have anything good happen," Violet said. "We must develop a plan, or we risk Doctor King panicking and killing Brianne."

"What do you have in mind?" I asked. "Personally, I'm completely happy to go right in there and kick the guy's butt. I don't want Brianne in his hands for a second longer than she has to be."

"Neither do I," Violet said. "However, I also do not want her killed because Doctor King panicked. I have an idea. Follow me."

The two of us made our way along Prince Albert Road until we reached Consort Lodge. It was an approximately eight story building, and if I had to guess, I would have said it was built in the 60s or 70s. It was made of a grey brick in the square, angulated architectural style of the time period. It certainly didn't look like much, but given the location, I had a sneaking suspicion that there wasn't a single apartment in here worth under two million pounds.

Violet and I made our way towards the front door, which was controlled by an electronic buzzer system.

"The flat owned by Doctor King is number eleven," Violet said, as she rang the bell for all of the apartments from one through ten.

"Yes?" A grumpy sounding elderly voice answered a moment later.

"Sorry to bother you, I've got delivery from Pizza Hut for unit six, but they're not answering," Violet said in a perfect English accent. "Mind buzzing me in?"

A moment later, the front door buzzed and I rushed forward and opened it. We were in! Now we just had to rescue Brianne.

CHAPTER 20

"So what's the plan now?" I asked. We were in the lobby, but as soon as we entered, Violet pulled me aside towards one of the far walls.

"I do not know if Doctor King has private cameras in this building," she said to me quietly. "We must be careful. If this is the area he uses to kill his victims, he may be more prudent than we expect him to be. We must err on the side of caution."

I nodded and pointed to the stairs, shrugging my shoulders. Violet nodded. The two of us slinked against the wall and made our way to the staircase, which had obviously not been renovated in quite some time.

"Good," Violet said, looking around. "In here, there do not appear to be any cameras. When we get to his floor, I want you to go to one end of the hallway and I will go to the other. On my phone, I have a program that allows me to falsify my number, and I will call

Doctor King pretending to be the hospital, telling him there is an emergency and that he is needed straight away. If we are lucky, he will come out of the apartment, and head towards one of us. Whichever one he comes to needs to call out, and the other will help to subdue him. If he goes to the elevators, we both tackle him."

"How on earth are we supposed to subdue a grown man?" I asked, looking at Violet's bag suspiciously. "You wouldn't happen to have your set of Tasers in there, would you?"

Violet gave me a coy smile as she reached into her purse and pulled one of her Tasers out, handing it to me. "I trust you still remember how to use this?"

"Yeah," I nodded. "I thought DCI Williams told you to get rid of these."

"He also thinks I should get rid of the police badge collection I keep. But they come in handy, and what DCI Williams does not know will not hurt him, as you say in English."

The part of me that had always followed the rules wanted to argue with Violet out of principle, but the part of me that wanted to make it out of here alive, and with Brianne safely rescued, was very happy to have the Tasers available.

"Okay," I said. "You take the far hallway, I'll take this end."

Violet nodded. "Let me make the phone call and then I go."

My heart pounded in my chest as Violet pulled out her phone, opened up an app, and tapped away at it for a moment before putting the phone to her ear.

"Yes, this is Nurse Stevens from the hospital. There's an emergency; a car accident with multiple casualties and we're all hands on deck right now. We need you to come back in."

I smiled; Nurse Stevens was the one who had told us about Doctor King outside the hospital that first day, and Violet did an excellent impression of her voice.

"I know you've just finished a long shift, but we really need you back in," Violet added. Apparently, Doctor King was not happy about this turn of events. "Right. See you soon."

Violet hung up the phone and raised her eyebrows at me. "Okay, now we see if he comes out."

I nodded, not trusting myself to talk. However, as Violet made her way down the hall, I couldn't help but think something was wrong. There was no sign of Doctor King coming out of his apartment, and after two minutes had passed, I started to get worried.

"We need to go in," I hissed to Violet as I made my way towards his apartment door, and Violet nodded.

"Yes, I agree. Something is definitely wrong."

I waited as Violet made her way to the front door and picked at the lock as quietly as possible. When, a moment later, I heard the familiar click of the latch coming undone, the two of us made our way into the apartment.

The apartment was classy, with neutral walls and a lot of medium shade wood trim. We entered into a small entry area, but from further down in the apartment, I could hear the muffled sounds of somebody calling for help.

There was absolutely no time to waste. I rushed forward, but Violet caught me by the arm and put a finger to her lips. This was obviously going to go a lot better if we managed to surprise Doctor King, so I moved more carefully, but quickly as I followed the sounds.

They were in the living room. The large space was sparsely decorated with midcentury furniture, and one wall was entirely covered in mirrors to make it look bigger than it actually was. On a yellow couch, Brianne was struggling, on her stomach, as Doctor King had one knee on her back and what appeared to be a tie wrapped around her neck.

Horrified, I jumped into action. Grabbing a large vase off a side table, I made my way towards Doctor King, intending to hit him over the head with it. I honestly wasn't even thinking about what might happen; I just wanted him to get off of Brianne.

What I hadn't expected was that at the last minute Doctor King noticed that I was coming, probably through that stupid mirror, and just as I reached up above me to hit him with the vase, he turned, let go of the tie, and punched me right in the stomach.

The wind was instantly knocked out of me, and I gasped for air as I dropped the vase to the ground and it shattered into a million pieces.

"Cassie!" Brianne called out hoarsely, gasping for breath. I was doubled over, struggling to breathe, and didn't even think of the Taser that was currently sitting in my back pocket.

Out of the corner of my eye, I suddenly saw a flash of movement, and shouted as I realized what it was. From underneath the couch, Doctor King had just pulled out a gun, but instead of shooting Brianne or aiming it at myself, he pointed it towards the door.

"Look out," I shouted at Violet just as the gun went off, and heard her falling to the ground.

This was definitely not good. Doctor King pointed the gun at me, and I froze for a split second, just like I had in the instant before the car hit me.

Only, this time, I wasn't going to get out of it with only a torn ACL and a fractured thumb.

The gun went off, and I closed my eyes, expecting the pain to hit me at any second, but instead I felt a whoosh of air about an inch from my face as Doctor King cried out in pain.

Opening my eyes, he clutched at his private area, swearing his head off.

"I'm going to make you pay for that," he said, pointing the gun at Brianne, but before he had a chance to I reacted. I wasn't about to let him hurt another one of my friends. I really hoped Violet was okay.

Lunging towards him, I let out a super awkward guttural roar, my hands reaching for the gun as I shoved him backwards. The two of us fell over the back arm of the couch, and I struggled to get away, yelling at Brianne to run for it.

Kicking at Doctor King, I managed to hit him right in the face and blood began to spurt from his nose. Out of the corner of my eye I could see Brianne had gotten up, and she was rushing towards Violet and the exit.

"Both of you, get out of here," I cried. I needed both of my friends to be safe. I needed them to get out, no matter what happened to me. Looking around frantically for the gun, I finally saw it, but it was too late. Doctor King had seen it too, and it was closer to him.

I made a split second decision. I could run for it as well, trying to get out the way I came in, which was the most direct route, or I could go the other way. The other way meant an unknown floor plan, it meant a longer route to the front door, but it also meant giving my friends a couple of extra seconds to get out of here.

In the end, it wasn't even a question what I was going to do.

I rushed as far away from where Violet and Brianne had been as possible, and heard a gunshot ring out once more. This time, one of the windows overlooking The Regent's Park shattered, and I covered my face as shards of glass came falling over me.

Turning, I looked to see where I was going to run, but found myself facing Doctor King stepping towards me, his gun raised.

"I never thought you were going to be more trouble than Violet," he snarled at me, all pretense of kindness gone from his face.

Suddenly, the snarl turned into a surprised look of shock as I heard the familiar tick of the Taser and he fell to the floor, completely unconscious.

"No one's ever more trouble than me," Violet replied. She held the Taser with both hands, and the front of her shirt was stained with blood.

As soon as she let go of the Taser, Violet fell to the floor, completely unconscious.

CHAPTER 21

"*B*rianne!" I called out, and a second later my friend poked her head around the corner.

"I'm here, what do you need?" she asked, her voice still quite hoarse.

Straight away my mind compartmentalized everything that needed to be done.

"Find a rope, or something, and tie up Doctor King. Make sure he's incapacitated."

"Can I just shoot him? That would save the taxpayers some money."

"I can't say I blame you if you did," I replied. "Personally, I'd rather see him rot in jail for everything he's ever done, plus if he's alive he can possibly tell us who his other victims were."

"You and your logic," Brianne muttered as she made her way towards the blinds and ripped the ropes off the side. Meanwhile, I pulled out my phone and dialed 999, and put it on speaker while pulling up the bottom of Violet's shirt to see what the damage was.

"I need an ambulance at 34 Prince Albert Road," I practically shouted into the phone. "Flat eleven. Now! I have a gunshot wound victim, and she's losing a *lot* of blood."

Violet's face was going white; she was obviously going into shock and I had to do whatever I could to save her life. Blood was pooling on the floor behind her, and given the location of the wound in her abdomen, I knew exactly what had been hit. It was her inferior vena cava, one of the major veins that took blood back to the right artery of the heart.

This was not good. There is absolutely no way Violet would be able to survive until she got to the hospital with this amount of blood loss.

"If he's not tied up yet, just shoot him," I said to Brianne, my voice surprisingly steady. "I need you to help me save Violet's life."

"Luckily for him, I just finished. What do you need?"

"A sewing kit, if possible. Sharp scissors. Nail ones, try the bathroom. If we're lucky, he'll actually have a medical kit somewhere."

Brianne nodded curtly and rushed away to find what I was after. I flipped Violet over, and confirmed that the bullet had gone straight through her, out the back. In this case, it was actually a good thing, because it meant I could access the vein that was hemorrhaging blood more easily than if I had to go in through the front.

A moment later, Brianne came back carrying a very well-stocked first aid kit. I supposed that was one advantage to being shot inside a doctor's home; a lot of us actually had a decent amount of medical equipment at home. I knew one cardiac surgeon when I was in medical school who actually kept a portable defibrillator in his entry closet in case someone ever had a heart attack while staying at his home.

"Clamp?" I asked, and Brianne passed over a small one.

"There's only one," she said, and I nodded.

"I need you to help me," I told Brianne. "Is there a scalpel?"

Brianne opened a scalpel still in its sterile wrapping and handed it over to me. I sliced open some of Violet's skin. It was definitely going to leave a bigger scar, but I figured if I managed to save her life she'd probably forgive me for it. Blood was seeping out of her at way too quick a rate for me to do anything else.

Reaching inside, I found the inferior vena cava, which, sure enough, had a giant, gaping hole in one side of it.

Using the clamp, I cut off the blood flow from the bottom. That way, no more blood was going to be able to get out.

"Check outside the window and see if the ambulance is here yet," I called out. "I also need you to call DCI Williams. His number is in my phone. Give him this address, tell him the serial killer is tied up in the apartment."

"Right away," Brianne said, standing up and making her way to the window to check for the ambulance's arrival. "They're not here yet."

I could feel Violet's pulse; it was definitely slowing down. I had to get this hole fixed, if nothing else. There was a very real possibility of some organ damage – given the location I suspected an intestine rupture at the very least – but at least the bleeding was stopping now that the clamp was in place. I pressed a finger into the hole to stop any more from coming out. There wasn't much more I could do right now without a surgical team and an operating room; the fact that there was a clamp in the doctor's first aid kit was already a huge help, otherwise I would have had to hold the vein closed myself.

Brianne picked my phone up off the ground and began going through my contacts. I could hear her calling DCI Williams while still checking for the ambulance every few seconds. I was definitely getting worried. Violet needed immediate medical attention, and she needed it now. I listened in the distance, and I began to hear sirens. Was that the paramedics now? Were they on their way?

"It sounds like they're coming," Brianne told me. "DCI Williams is on his way too to take care of this piece of scum," she added, kicking at Doctor King with her toe. He let out a small groan but didn't move; Violet had evidently done a number on him with that Taser.

"I hope so," I said. "She needs a surgeon straight away."

"You've done a bloody good job yourself," Brianne said, shaking her head.

"I hope you don't mean that literally," I said, looking around at all the blood. This apartment definitely looked like a crime scene, now. Violet needed blood, and fast.

I looked at the first aid kit.

"Brianne?"

"Yes?"

"I need you to look through that kit and see if there's a needle in there. I need to transfer my blood over to Violet."

"You're O negative?" Brianne asked, and I nodded.

"No. O positive. Which gives me an eighty-two percent chance of being able to give Violet my blood, but if I don't do it, she's going to die. You're not O-negative, are you?"

Brianne shook her head. "Sorry. AB positive. I'm basically the most useless person in this situation." She made her way back to the first aid kit and began rummaging through it. "There's a syringe here, but it means you're going to have to share it."

"If Violet has any blood transferable diseases I'm

pretty sure I already have it," I replied, looking at the immense amount of blood that was now all over my arms. "I need to keep this hole plugged. You're going to have to do it."

"Right," Brianne said, making her way over to me. Wrapping a piece of plastic tubing around my arm, she tapped at my veins a couple of times, then stuck the syringe in, pulling up the tube and filling it with blood. It was actually a pretty big tube, probably 50ml, which was more than I would have expected. I winced slightly at the poke of the needle, but Brianne had good aim, and I barely felt it.

Pulling the syringe out of my arm, she pulled Violet's arm over, searching for a vein or artery to put the blood into. Her veins were hiding though; the blood loss didn't make it easy. Eventually, Brianne found one on the top of her hand.

"At least she's not going to be able to feel this," Brianne said as she injected the blood into Violet.

"Again," I said as soon as she was done. "Keep doing it until the ambulance gets here."

Brianne managed to transfer four syringes worth, or about half a unit of blood, before the sound of the sirens got close enough that I ordered her to go downstairs and open the door for the EMTs.

There was a chance that Violet was going to have a bad reaction to the blood, but I really hoped she didn't. She certainly didn't look like she had the chills or anything like that, which was a good sign.

Two minutes later, Brianne came rushing back in, followed by three paramedics carrying a stretcher.

"I'm holding the hole in her inferior vena cava shut," I told them. "I've transferred half a unit of my blood into her, but I'm not sure her blood type. I'm O positive. I'm going to keep holding the hole shut, and I'm coming with you."

"Right, let's get her to the hospital as quickly as possible," one of the paramedics said, with one grabbing her shoulders and the other her legs. "There's only the one wound?"

"As far as I know," I replied. The paramedics counted to three and moved Violet onto the stretcher. Straight away, the four of us rushed back out to the ambulance.

"Let's put her on her side," one of the paramedics said as the ambulance sped away. "I want to give her some oxygen."

In a twist of irony, University Hospital where Doctor King worked was the closest hospital, and it was where we ended up. As soon as we got there a surgical team was already ready - I had heard one of the EMTs on the radio calling for them to be ready when we got there back at Doctor King's apartment - and a nurse quickly took over for me holding the hole shut while they wheeled Violet away to the operating room.

I was mostly in a daze as I made my way to the waiting area. I barely even noticed the stares from people who must have wondered if I should be locked up in a mental hospital. I was sure I was covered in blood, I was pretty sure my head wound had re-opened at some point during the ruckus, and my thousand-yard-stare would have driven most people away screaming.

I was basically the bad guy in a zombie movie right now.

I really hoped it wasn't too late for Violet.

CHAPTER 22

About twenty minutes later, after a nurse appeared and made sure I didn't need medical attention myself – my head wound was oozing slightly but it wasn't fully open – Brianne showed up, along with DCI Williams. She handed me my phone, which I had completely forgotten to grab in all the chaos, and I found myself immediately texting Jake to come over.

"I'm going to need a statement from you, when you're up to it," DCI Williams told me, and I nodded.

"Has he been arrested?"

"He has. I would have arrived sooner if someone hadn't commandeered my police car."

I gave DCI Williams a sheepish look. "I didn't realize Violet was going to do that, in my defense. I thought she was going to wait for you, too."

"Well, it's done now. The important thing is we've

got a killer off the streets. Come by the station later and I'll take your statement. I've got Brianne's, already."

I nodded and thanked DCI Williams. "I'll let you know if Violet's alright," I told him.

"She will be," he replied.

"You didn't see her."

"No, but she always is."

I wished I had that kind of confidence. As DCI Williams left, I plopped myself back down on the chair, next to Brianne.

"*Now* you look like a crazy person," Brianne informed me, and I couldn't help it. I laughed, in spite of the seriousness of the situation.

"Are you alright?" I asked her. A bruise was forming on her neck, but she nodded.

"I'm shaken up. There's probably going to be a few nightmares in my immediate future, but I'm alive, thanks to you and Violet."

"Brianne, I'm so sorry. I never meant for you to get involved in this. I never meant for him to come after *you*. It was supposed to be me."

"No, don't," Brianne said, shaking her head. "It's not your fault."

"It is, though. If I hadn't come to see you, he never would have targeted you."

"Nope. It's *his* fault for being a serial killing piece of excrement. Trust me. I don't blame you in the slightest. But you did save my life, and for that, I'm eternally grateful."

"Why did you get into the car with him, anyway?" I asked. "Did he threaten you?"

"Yup," Brianne nodded. "He pulled a gun on me. Pointed it at me through the car window, told me if I didn't get in he was going to shoot me right there in the street."

I shook my head, incredulous. "What a horrible person."

"Exactly. When you called, he told me to answer, and to act natural, or he was going to shoot me right then and there."

"When you changed a few of those facts around, that was when I knew something was wrong," I said, and Brianne nodded.

"The fact that you might pick those up was the only chance I had. After I hung up, he got me to throw the phone out the window so that I couldn't be tracked with it."

"Violet found it; she hacked your iCloud and used it to try and find you, which at least put us in the right area."

"I'm so glad you did," Brianne said, and a moment later a nurse came out and looked at the two of us.

"Which one of you is Brianne? The police detective has ordered me to have a look at you; your injuries need to be recorded as well."

I looked over as my friend got up. "I'd give you a hug, but I'm pretty disgusting right now."

"That's okay, I've had better days too," Brianne said with a wink as she followed the nurse down the hall.

I leaned back in my chair, finding myself completely exhausted, and closed my eyes. I didn't realize I had dozed off until I opened them later and found Jake sitting next to me.

"How long have you been there?" I asked.

"About half an hour," he replied. "You looked so peaceful I thought I would just let you sleep."

"I'm pretty sure nothing about what I look like right now is peaceful," I laughed. "Sorry about the serial killer look."

"I heard from the nurse that you got your serial killer."

"It was Doctor King," I nodded. "Violet figured it out. He kidnapped Brianne, and shot Violet. All of this is her blood."

"Is she going to be all right?"

"I have no idea. She got taken to surgery as soon as we got here, and I haven't heard anything since."

"Well, let me convince the nurse to let you into the staff showers, get you some new clothes, and while you're doing that I'll go out and get you a burger."

I smiled gratefully at Jake. "I knew I loved you for a reason."

〜

*F*our hours later Violet came out of surgery, alive. It had been a close one, according to the surgeon, and he told me that if it wasn't for my quick thinking and reactions, Violet would absolutely be dead by now. Jake had gone back to work after two hours; with the killer caught, the police were now bugging him for the final report on Marnie Phillips's autopsy, so when Violet woke up, I was the only person in the room.

"Has he been arrested?" was the first thing she asked.

"Yeah," I replied. "Thanks to you."

Violet simply nodded and then drifted back off to sleep. I smiled and tucked the blanket back in under her.

≈

*F*orty-eight hours later Violet was released from the hospital, insisting that she was fine despite the fact that her doctors wanted to keep her there for another few days under observation.

"I will have Cassie come by every few hours to check on me," Violet insisted. "You know she is a good doctor, she is the one who saved my life."

Eventually, the doctors relented, and that was how I found myself helping Violet out of the cab as she winced; her abdominal muscles had taken a beating from the bullet, not to mention her insides. And surgery wasn't exactly a super fun thing to deal with either.

"I swear, if I see you leave this house, I will hunt you down and I will take you back to the hospital myself," I threatened. "And I've called Mrs. Michaels and told her what's going on; she's going to look out for you too, and you know old people love spying on their neighbors."

"I am fine," Violet replied.

"Is that why you can't even get out of the car on your own? You are not fine, and you're going to rest. Besides, it's Christmas Eve. Even the world's greatest detective can take a week off at Christmas."

"The criminals do not do so, so why would I?"

"Because you were shot and almost died. If you go out and bleed to death in the street like an idiot, I'm going to be really mad at you. Now, get in the house, and let me go get your Christmas present."

I helped Violet up the stairs, settled her on the couch, then ran home and grabbed the copies of *The Strand* that I had found for her. By the time I got back into the house, I found Violet mulling around the kitchen, trying to make a smoothie.

"Out," I ordered, pointing back to the couch. "Go sit on that, and open this. I'll make your smoothie for you. I *will* move in here and for a few days with you if I need to."

Violet scowled, but did as I ordered, taking the

wrapped pile of magazines from me and making her way back to the couch.

As I put ingredients in the blender, I could hear her unwrapping the magazines, and she burst out laughing when she finally saw what they were.

"You do have a good sense of irony," Violet said. "Did you buy these before, or after Marnie Phillips's murder?"

"After," I replied. "But I figured the world's greatest real detective would enjoy some original copies of the world's greatest fictional detective."

"I do love it," Violet said. "Since I am certain you would not like me getting it myself, if you go upstairs into my room you will find your present on the dresser."

I didn't like going into Violet's room at all; this house was filled with weird and creepy stuff; I had once come across a Komodo Dragon in her bedroom.

"Is there anything that might kill me upstairs?"

"Plenty of things, but so long as you simply go to the bedroom and get your gift off the dresser, I believe you will be fine."

I made my way up, and sure enough, found a small box, wrapped absolutely beautifully, sitting on Violet's dresser. Of course even she could wrap presents perfectly.

Making my way downstairs, I smiled at her. "Thanks for this."

"Open it."

I sat down on the couch across from her and pulled open the wrapping paper. Inside was a box labelled 'ERKA'.

I opened the box, and found nestled perfectly, like it was in a jewelry box, the nicest stethoscope I had ever seen.

"They are from Germany. My source tells me it is the best stethoscope money can buy."

"Thank you," I said almost breathlessly, touching the stethoscope lightly, as though it were glass. "But I don't know if I'm going to be a doctor yet."

"You do know, I think," Violet said, and I looked at her, questions in my eyes.

"I spoke with Brianne, when I was at the hospital. I wanted her to come and see me. After all, she would not leave the apartment without me when you told her to run, and I thought that was quite brave of her. She told me what you did. She told me that you are the reason I am here today, and that you even had her transfer some of your blood into me so that I would survive."

"Still, that doesn't mean I'm going to be a doctor. It just means I didn't want my best friend to die."

"No, but your presence of mind in that situation, it was something. And it is not the first time I have seen it. You have helped me when I had been stabbed. I have seen it. You are at your best when you are in an emergency situation and someone requires medical attention. You do not panic. You are focused, and clear-headed, and calm. You make everyone around you calmer for it, and you will eventually realize that is what you were meant to do."

I sat on the couch, staring at the gorgeous stethoscope, as tears came unwillingly to my eyes. Violet was right. Of course Violet was right. The answer had been staring me in the face the entire time. The things that made me an excellent surgeon were also going to make me an excellent emergency doctor. That was what I was meant to do.

A huge wave of relief came over me. I knew what I was going to do. I knew what I *had* to do. There was absolutely no doubt about it in my mind anymore. I was going to medical school. I was going to finish my studies to become a doctor. And I was going to save people's lives in emergency situations. That was what I was best at. That was what I was meant to do.

This was definitely the best Christmas I'd had in a long time. How far I'd come in less than a year.

ALSO BY SAMANTHA SILVER

First of all, I wanted to thank you for reading my book. I well and truly hope you enjoyed reading this book as much as I loved writing it.

If you enjoyed Killed in King's Cross I'd really appreciate it if you could take a moment and leave a review for the book on Amazon, to help other readers find the book as well.

Other Cassie Coburn Mysteries

Poison in Paddington (Cassie Coburn Mystery #1)

Bombing in Belgravia (Cassie Coburn Mystery #2)

Strangled in Soho (Cassie Coburn Mystery #4)

Stabbed in Shoreditch (Cassie Coburn Mystery #5)

Killed in King's Cross (Cassie Coburn Mystery #6)

Ruby Bay Mysteries

Death Down Under (Ruby Bay Mystery #1)

Arson in Australia (Ruby Bay Mystery #2)

The Killer Kangaroo (Ruby Bay Mystery #3)

Western Woods Mysteries

Back to Spell One (Western Woods Mystery #1)

Two Peas in a Potion (Western Woods Mystery #2)

Three's a Coven (Western Woods Mystery #3)

Four Leaf Clovers (Western Woods Mystery #4)

Magical Bookshop Mysteries

Alice in Murderland (Magical Bookshop Mystery #1)

Murder on the Oregon Express (Magical Bookshop Mystery #2)

The Very Killer Caterpillar (Magical Bookshop Mystery #3)

Death Quixote (Magical Bookshop Mystery #4)

Pride and Premeditation (Magical Bookshop Mystery #5)

Willow Bay Witches Mysteries

The Purr-fect Crime (Willow Bay Witches #1)

Barking up the Wrong Tree (Willow Bay Witches #2)

Just Horsing Around (Willow Bay Witches #3)

Lipstick on a Pig (Willow Bay Witches #4)

A Grizzly Discovery (Willow Bay Witches #5)

Sleeping with the Fishes (Willow Bay Witches #6)

Get your Ducks in a Row (Willow Bay Witches #7)

Busy as a Beaver (Willow Bay Witches #8)

Moonlight Cove Mysteries

Witching Aint's Easy (Moonlight Cove Mystery #1)

Witching for the Best (Moonlight Cove Mystery #2)

ABOUT THE AUTHOR

Samantha Silver lives in British Columbia, Canada, along with her husband and a little old doggie named Terra. She loves animals, skiing and of course, writing cozy mysteries.

Made in the USA
Las Vegas, NV
04 May 2024

89541805R00111